Gun Law at Lost Bucket

A quiet life is the only thing Dane Cleadon wants, but it seems he can't escape his past reputation as a gun fighter and town tamer. When he is called out by young Tim Ryland, he does his best to avoid trouble but to no avail. Ryland dies accidentally by his own gun and his father, local magnate Cass Ryland, wants revenge. Still hoping to avert bloodshed, Cleadon leaves town accompanied by his friend Cayuse, another old timer. They are pursued by Ryland and his gang into the hills where they stumble upon a ghost town by the name of Lost Bucket. What grisly fate befell the prospectors who built it? And is there a connection to Ryland? In seeking the answers, Cleadon must rely one more time on his guns.

Gun Law at Lost Bucket

Colin Bainbridge

A Black Horse Western

ROBERT HALE

© Colin Bainbridge 2020
First published in Great Britain 2020

ISBN 978-0-7198-3077-8

The Crowood Press
The Stable Block
Crowood Lane
Ramsbury
Marlborough
Wiltshire SN8 2HR

www.bhwesterns.com

Robert Hale is an imprint
of The Crowood Press

Typeset by
Derek Doyle & Associates, Shaw Heath
Printed and bound in Great Britain by
4Bind Ltd, Stevenage, SG1 2XT

CHAPTER ONE

Old 'Cayuse' Norman had just finished his second helping of apple pie and his third cup of coffee when he glanced out of the dining-room window.

'Uh huh,' he muttered. 'Looks like trouble is headed this way.'

'Trouble?' his companion replied.

'Take a look yourself, Cleadon.'

The other man leaned over.

'Ain't that the young whippersnapper you had to slap down just the other day?' Cayuse queried.

Cleadon let out a sigh.

'Seems like.'

'Maybe he'll just pass on by.'

'Somehow I doubt it.'

Cleadon sat back again. After a few moments the door of the dining room flew open and the youngster stepped through. Cleadon took a sip of coffee. It had gone cold.

'Cleadon!'

The youth's voice was taut and shrill. Cleadon took another sip before looking up.

'I figured it wouldn't take long to find you,' the youngster said.

'I'm easy to find, but why would anyone be lookin'?'

'You know why.'

Cleadon let out a sigh.

'Look son,' he said. 'We've been through this once already. Why don't you just turn round and leave? Or better still, sit down and have a cup of coffee. On me. This here's kinda cold now. Let me order some fresh.'

'I'd take up his offer,' Cayuse said.

For a moment the youngster seemed to hesitate before taking another step forward.

'Come on, old man,' he said. 'I'm givin' you a chance.' He clapped his hands together and then held his arms wide.

'They tell me you used to be good. I say they're lyin'.'

Cleadon and Cayuse were the only ones left in the dining room. Ava, the proprietor, had gone back in the kitchen and Cleadon was hoping she would stay there.

'I think we've already had this conversation,' Cleadon replied.

'You tried to make me look a fool. I don't take that from anyone.'

'So what's this really about?'

The young man licked his lips.

'I say you're a coward,' he muttered.

'Maybe I'm just someone who's lookin' for a bit of peace and quiet,' Cleadon said.

'You're a coward now, and I figure you always have been.'

'How would you know one way or the other?' Cayuse said. 'You're too young for anythin'.'

'I ain't too young!' the kid exploded. 'Come on, then. I'll take you both on.' Immediately the words were out of his mouth his gun was in his hand and spitting lead and flame as the afternoon silence exploded in a deluge of noise. The bullet whistled between Cleadon and Cayuse and buried itself in the back wall of the eating house. Cayuse flinched slightly, but Cleadon remained unmoved.

'Come on,' the youngster yelled, waving his gun in the air. Out of the corner of his eye, Cleadon saw Ava emerge from the kitchen.

'Not in here,' he said. 'Let's settle this outside.'

The young man was confused. He looked from Cleadon to the woman and back again.

'Put your gun in its holster,' Cleadon said. 'That way we can prove who's the faster draw. If that's really what you want.'

Cayuse glanced at him and seemed about to say something, but Cleadon silenced him with a look. The youngster stood undecided, but after a few moments he did as Cleadon suggested.

'Come on then,' he breathed. 'Let's go outside.'

7

Cleadon slowly got to his feet.

'You go first,' the youngster said.

He was agitated, but stepped slightly to one side to let Cleadon pass. As Cleadon did so, he suddenly swung with his right fist. The blow caught the youngster on the side of his head and knocked him back against one of the tables. Quickly, Cleadon raised his fist again but the years had slowed him and the young man was able to move aside. In a moment his gun was in his hand again and he opened fire. Cleadon felt the bullet slice across his cheek before he succeeded in grasping hold of his assailant's wrist. For a few moments they wrestled grimly before they both fell to the ground. As they did so the gun exploded once again. Cayuse had got to his feet and let out a gasp. Without thinking he moved forwards, fearing the worst, but when the two men came apart it was the youngster who lay inert, blood oozing from his chest.

'Cleadon,' he gasped. 'Are you hurt?'

Cleadon was out of breath. He shook his head as he knelt beside the body. Ava, who had been cowering behind the counter since emerging from the kitchen, came over to join them.

'Is he . . .?' she began.

Cleadon glanced up at her.

'He's dead,' he confirmed. Slowly and painfully he staggered to his feet.

'I'm sorry about this,' he said.

'What have you got to be sorry about?' she

8

replied. 'None of it was your fault.'

'It sure wasn't,' Cayuse said. 'Hell, Cleadon ain't even carryin' a gun!'

'I thought I could lay him out,' Cleadon responded. 'I thought I might be able to disarm him.'

'He was askin' for it,' Cayuse replied. 'You got nothin' to blame yourself for.'

Cleadon made a gesture.

'It's so stupid,' he said. 'He's only a kid.'

'He's old enough to have caused a heap of trouble round these parts,' Ava put in.

Cleadon turned to face her.

'You know him?' he said.

'Sure. I'm surprised you don't.'

'Cleadon likes to keep himself to himself,' Cayuse interposed.

'Yeah,' Ava replied. 'I've noticed.'

'Do you know who he is?' Cleadon asked Cayuse.

'I keep out of things, too,' Cayuse replied. He paused before continuing: 'I've heard some stuff. I didn't give it any heed. He ain't the only kid who's full of hell.'

'Go on then,' Cleadon said to Ava. 'Tell me.' Ava exchanged glances with Cayuse. Cayuse's face was blank.

'I might be wrong. But I'm pretty sure that's Tim Ryland. Cass Ryland's son.'

It was clear that her words meant nothing to Cleadon.

'Cass Ryland,' she continued. 'The owner of the

biggest ranch around these parts, the Hat R.'
Cleadon remained uncomprehending, but Cayuse
seemed to understand.

'It's easy to see you ain't been too long in these
parts, Cleadon,' he said. 'Or maybe it's because
Cass Ryland and his crew keep themselves pretty
much to themselves. At least as far as this place is
concerned. It's kinda unusual to see anyone from
the Hat R here in town.'

'There's a reason for that,' Ava put in. 'From
what I've heard, Cass Ryland as good as owns Blue
Bluff. If the boys from the Hat R want to let off
some steam, that's where they head for, not here.
It's where Cass gets his supplies.'

Cleadon didn't seem to be taking too much
notice of what Ava was telling him. Instead he
glanced down at the lifeless body of the youngster.

'Better get the marshal and the undertaker,' he
said. At his words, Ava went out into the street,
returning again almost immediately.

'I've sent someone,' she said. 'I didn't go into
details.'

'You ain't got nothin' to worry about,' Cayuse
said. 'Me and Ava are witnesses to what happened.
It was an accident. You acted in pure self-defence.'

Ava looked uneasy.

'Cleadon might not have anything to fear from the
law,' she said, 'but Cass Ryland is a different matter.'

'How's that?' Cayuse queried.

'Cass Ryland is a hard man. He isn't going to take

10

the death of his son lightly, no matter how it happened. If you want my opinion, he's going to be out for revenge.' Cleadon was thoughtful.

'How far is the Hat R?' he said.

'About fifteen miles. Towards Blue Bluff.'

'That won't take me too long.'

'What do you mean?' Cayuse said.

'Cass Ryland needs to be told what happened.'

'Leave that to the marshal,' Ava said.

'Nope, I don't think I can do that. I figure I owe it to Cass Ryland.'

'You're talkin' crazy,' Cayuse said.

'Cayuse is right,' Ava responded. 'Cass and his boys have got a reputation for being mean. That's how he built up the Hat R. Don't expect him to see sense. If you go ridin' in there, I wouldn't give much for your chances of ridin' back out again.'

'If you ask me, it'd be downright foolhardy to go anywhere near the Hat R.'

'I'll take my chances,' Cleadon replied. 'I sure appreciate your concern, but it's something I've just got to do.'

Before the others had time to expostulate further, the door opened and the marshal came in. He glanced at the body before looking up at Ava.

'You'd better tell me what happened,' he said.

Cleadon had intended to ride over to the Hat R that same day, but by the time the official procedures had been carried out, it was late in the

11

evening when he and Cayuse left the marshal's office. Marshal Dunbar had added his voice to those of Ava and Cayuse in an effort to persuade him otherwise, but he had remained fixed in his purpose.

'I can't stop you ridin' out there,' the marshal said, 'but I warn you, Cass Ryland can be a dangerous man. I wouldn't want to have to deal with another killing.'

'It wasn't a killing,' Cayuse put in. 'It was plumb accidental.'

'OK, but you understand what I'm sayin'?'

'I understand,' Cleadon said.

'But you won't change your mind?'

'Nope. I'm sorry. I appreciate your concern and I'll be careful, but I'm goin' ahead.'

'Then I'll ride out with you,' the marshal said.

'Me too,' Cayuse added.

'Again, I thank you for your offer, but this is my problem. It's somethin' that I have to deal with myself.'

'You don't owe that young punk nothin',' Cayuse said. The marshal looked closely at Cleadon.

'You say this was the second time young Ryland approached you?' he said.

'Approached is the wrong word,' Cayuse interrupted. 'Both times he was downright aggressive. He was just spoilin' for a fight.'

'And why was that?'

'Why? You must have heard of Dane Cleadon?

12

Hell, he was the fastest gun around. He cleaned up more lawless towns than. . . .'

'That's enough,' Cleadon said. He turned to the marshal.

'It was all a long time ago,' he said. 'I thought I'd put all that behind me.' The marshal looked from Cleadon to Cayuse and back again.

'You don't have to tell me,' he said. 'I'm only raisin' the question for form's sake. I know about Dane Cleadon as much as the next man. Or at least as much as most lawmen. I just didn't figure he was livin' right here in town.'

'I was hopin' my reputation wouldn't have followed me this time. Looks like I was mistaken,' Cleadon said.

'I wonder how young Ryland got to hear about it?' the marshal said.

'I don't know,' Cleadon replied. 'It's the last thing I would have wanted. I've had more than enough of that kind of thing. But it seems like when you finally seem to have put the past behind you, there's one more whippersnapper hell bent on bringin' it up again, tryin' to make a name for themselves.'

'When will they ever learn?' the marshal mused.

'I'm beginnin' to wish things had been different,' Cleadon said. 'Maybe I took a wrong turn somewhere along the line, maybe. . . .'

'You got nothin' to blame yourself for,' Cayuse put in.

13

'Cayuse is right,' Dunbar said. 'Things were a lot different then. There were no rules. Things were wild. It was every man for himself. Folks needed people like you to bring some sort of law and order.'

'I don't know,' Cleadon said, 'but when I hung up my guns – a long time ago – I never figured on somethin' like this.'

'I still have to wear mine,' the marshal said. 'And by the way, that hothead Ryland was breakin' the law himself. There's an ordinance against carryin' firearms in town.'

'Pity not everyone obeys it,' Cayuse muttered.

The sun had not long risen when Cleadon set off for the Hat R. During a restless night he had gone over everything that had happened, but he had not changed his mind. Despite what everyone had said, he still felt an obscure sense of guilt. He couldn't help but feel that he owed it to Cass Ryland to tell him personally what had happened. It was a cool, bright morning, the sort of day Cleadon would normally have enjoyed. As things were, sunk in thought, he took little notice of his surroundings or of how long he had been riding. It was the attitude of his horse which brought him round from his reverie and made him aware of the presence of cattle. They were standing singly and in little groups, and they appeared sleek and well fed. He took a closer look. The Hat R brand was burned on their hides. He must be on Hat R range, and this was confirmed presently when he saw three riders in the distance coming towards him.

Their presence made no particular impression till another pair of horsemen appeared to his left. As they got closer, one of the newcomers shouted something. It wasn't clear whether the man was shouting at him or the other riders, but as the two groups converged, it became clear that their intentions were not friendly. It didn't bother Cleadon too much. Since there was no point in trying to evade them, he drew his horse to a halt and taking out his tobacco pouch, commenced to roll a cigarette. The second two riders came up alongside him. They had guns in their hands.

'Get down off your horse and unbuckle your gunbelt!' one of them snapped.

'I don't want any trouble,' he replied.

'Shut up and do as I say,' the man ordered.

Cleadon put the cigarette in his top pocket before holding out his arms so that his jacket fell open.

'As you can see, I'm not wearin' a gunbelt.'

The man took a close look before glancing at his companion in some confusion.

'I'm not carryin' arms. I'm here because I've got a message for Cass Ryland. I take it you're some of his men.'

Before either man could reply, the other group of riders came up. In the lead was a man thin and sharp as a knife blade riding a big palomino.

'I'll handle this,' he said. Cleadon looked him closely up and down. He didn't like what he saw.

'What in hell are you doin'?' he said. 'This is private property.'

'I didn't see any sign.'

'Don't need any sign. Everyone knows strangers ain't allowed on Hat R land.'

'Like I was sayin' to your friend here,' Cleadon replied, nodding in the direction of the first man. 'I don't want to cause any bother. I would just appreciate the chance to have a word with your boss.'

'You got a nerve. What makes you think Cass Ryland would be interested in anythin' you got to say?'

'All the same, I'd like to speak with him.' One of the riders coughed.

'Why don't you just let me finish him off now, Seb?' he muttered. Seb turned towards him. For a moment he looked angry, but the frown quickly faded from his features.

'That's a mighty good idea,' he replied. 'But the way I figure it, shootin' him would be just too easy. How about we have a little fun first?'

'What you got in mind?' someone shouted. Before Cleadon could say anything a lariat suddenly snaked out and he found himself pinioned.

'All right,' Seb shouted. 'Make sure he's fastened tight.' His words were greeted with loud whoops. A couple of the riders swung and tied Cleadon to the cantle of Seb's saddle.

'OK boys!' he shouted. 'Let's take a ride.'

He dug his spurs into the palomino's flanks and the horse lurched forwards. The other four riders followed, laughing and whooping as Cleadon was dragged along. The palomino picked up speed and Cleadon could do nothing but grit his teeth against the pain, and struggle to remain conscious as his head hit the turf. The ordeal seemed to last an eternity before suddenly the ground ceased to hurtle by beneath him and he came to a jerking halt. The man called Seb reined in his horse and turned to the others.

'Unfasten him.'

'You lettin' him go?' Seb laughed.

'What do you think?' He nodded towards a nearby tree.

'A necktie party!' someone yelled. Cleadon was dragged to his feet. Amidst an uproar of shouting and jeering he was pushed and hauled till he stood beneath an overhanging branch.

'Put him on a horse,' Seb commanded. One of the men dismounted. In a moment Cleadon was seized by the shoulders and manhandled aboard the horse. He ached, and blood was flowing down his left arm. He was in no condition to put up any sort of fight. All he could do was utter a silent prayer and turn his face to the sky as one of the men advanced to tie a rope around his neck. The moment he did so he heard the loud crack of a rifle, and one of the men fell heavily from his saddle. The scene was transformed in an instant into one of panic and confusion. Another shot rang out, and a third. A second man fell, and one of the men's horses bolted and went galloping off. The effect on Cleadon was to clear his senses. He half climbed and half fell from the saddle and as he did so he heard running footsteps and a voice call:

'Here! Take this!'

A six-gun was placed in his hand. He turned to face his remaining assailants but there was no need. The rest of them, Seb included, had turned to flee and were already out of range. He felt faint and, breathing heavily, leaned against the tree. Through a kind of mist he saw a figure next to him, a figure he recognized.

'Cayuse,' he murmured. 'What in tarnation are you doin' here?' Cayuse didn't reply. Instead he moved quickly to where the two men he had shot lay on the ground.

'One of them is only wounded,' he said. As if in response the man began to moan. Cayuse quickly got to his feet and came back to where Cleadon was still propped against the tree.

'They were goin' to lynch me!' he said.

'Yeah.' Cayuse regarded Cleadon closely.

'I saw what else they did,' he said. 'Pity I couldn't have made it any quicker. As it is I only just got here in the nick of time.' With some effort, Cleadon managed to stand upright.

'Look,' Cayuse said. 'We need to get you to a doc. More importantly right now, we need to get out of here. Those varmints have only been scared off temporarily. They'll be back pretty soon lookin' to finish off what they started, aimin' to finish off both of us. Do you think you can ride?' Cleadon nodded.

'Sure,' he said. 'I'll be all right.'

'Just give me a few moments till I round up your horse,' Cayuse replied.

It was quickly done. With Cayuse's help, Cleadon hoisted himself into the saddle. Cayuse was looking anxiously around, but as yet there was no sign of any riders. Without more ado he stepped into leather and they both set off, quickly spurring their horses to a gallop. Cleadon hurt from head to toe, but nothing seemed to be broken. He gritted his teeth and they carried on riding. The number of cattle began to dwindle, but it wasn't till the last of them were a long way behind that they slowed to a trot, feeling fairly sure they had left the Hat R range and were safe from pursuit. It was clear to Cayuse that Cleadon needed to take a break, so he led the way into a grove of trees where he dismounted and then helped the oldster from the saddle. Propping Cleadon's head against a fallen stump, he rummaged in his saddle-bags and produced a battered metal flask.

'Here,' he said, holding it out to Cleadon. 'Take a few swigs of this. It should help.'

Cleadon took the flask and tilted it back. Almost

19

as soon as the whiskey hit the back of his throat, he felt better. For the first time Cayuse noticed that the sleeve of Cleadon's jacket was soaked in blood.

'Let me take a look at that,' he said. He helped Cleadon take off his jacket and shirt. His body was cut and bruised and his shoulder was badly scraped, but there didn't seem to be anything more serious.

'I figure you're gonna be plumb sore for a while,' he said. He went back to his horse, and this time retrieved a bottle from his saddle-bags. He took off his neckerchief and poured some liquid from the bottle on to it.

'I'm afraid this is gonna hurt,' he said. Cleadon grinned and took another swig of the whiskey.

'Go right ahead,' he replied. Cayuse began to dab the liquid on to the most obvious of Cleadon's abrasions, finishing with his shoulder.

'What the hell've you got in there,' Cleadon asked through gritted teeth. Cayuse shrugged.

'Your guess is as good as mine,' he said. 'Bought it at a medicine show. Seems to work, though.' When he had finished Cleadon pulled his shirt back on.

'I guess I owe you,' he said.

'None of us was too happy about you settin' off for the Hat R on your own. I figured it might be an idea to follow you.'

'Us?'

'Me, the marshal, Ava. I figure you know that.' Cleadon handed the flask back to Cayuse.

'Take a drop yourself,' he said.

'Fact of the matter is,' Cayuse continued after swallowing a mouthful, 'we were a mite untruthful when we told you about Cass Ryland. He's got an even worse reputation than we were allowing for.'

'I think I can vouch for that now,' Cleadon replied. Cayuse grinned.

'Come on,' he said, 'let's get you to the doc.' Cleadon nodded, but seemed reluctant to get back on his feet.

'What are we waitin' for?' Cayuse asked.

'I'm tryin' to think,' Cleadon said.

'What's there to think about?'

'I'm thinkin' about what you just said. About the marshal and Ava.'

'What about them?'

'This isn't going to be the last of this affair,' Cleadon said. 'I think I can see things a little more clearly now. There's no way Ryland is going to accept the death of his son. Maybe he'd be right. But he's going to be looking for revenge. Even more so now that one of his men has been killed. He's gonna be lookin' for me, and anyone whose got any connection with me is liable to come under threat.'

'So what are you sayin'?'

'I'm sayin' that the only sensible thing for me to do is to get out of town and move on. It ain't like I've been around long enough to put down roots.'

'I don't know about that,' Cayuse replied. 'Quite

a few folk have taken a shining to you.'

'All the more reason not to put anyone else's life in danger.'

'You're in no condition to do anything much at the moment,' Cayuse said.

'I'll be fine. I don't object to seein' a doc, but once I've done that I figure I'll just collect a few things and be on my way. Light a shuck, quiet and easy. I don't want to make something of it. You can explain how it is later, if you like.'

'I won't be doin' that,' Cayuse said.

'What do you mean? Why not?'

'Because I'll be comin' with you,' Cayuse replied. Cleadon was about to laugh, but the impulse quickly passed.

'What are you talkin' about? You can't do that?'

'Why not? I figure I've been around these parts for long enough. Besides, I'm the one who killed the varmint that tried to lynch you. Cass Ryland will be lookin' out for me too.'

'Nobody would have recognized you.'

'I wouldn't be too sure of that.'

For a few moments neither of them said anything further. They took a few more sips from the flask, after which Cleadon began to struggle to his feet. Cayuse made to help him but he waved him aside.

'I'm feelin' a lot better already,' he said. He walked unsteadily to his horse and managed to climb into the saddle.

'Don't go overdoin' things,' Cayuse said. 'You're

not as young as you used to be.'

With a final look around to make sure there were still no signs of pursuit, they spurred their horses forwards. It didn't take long till they arrived at Cleadon's isolated shack at the edge of town. They came to a halt and led the horses to a rough stable at the rear. Cleadon was feeling beat, and Cayuse volunteered to go for the doc. When he got back, however, he was by himself; the doctor was out.

'Maybe it's just as well,' Cleadon said. 'I don't know exactly why, but I've a feelin' that the fewer people know about this, the better.'

'You need some attention.'

'You seem to have done a pretty good job. Just let me lie down for a spell.'

While Cleadon rested in an adjoining room, Cayuse sat on the veranda and rolled a cigarette. The sun was sinking low. He lit up and took the smoke deep into his lungs. He stretched out his legs and looked up. A few wisps of cloud drifted across the sky. He found himself in a reflective mood. Cleadon had been so close to being killed. If he had arrived on the scene only seconds later . . .

It seemed that all the rumours about Cass Ryland might be true: how he had forced smaller ranches to sell at low prices, how he had been suspected of cattle rustling to build his own herd. And other things. Certainly, if a man acquired a ranch the size of the Hat R, seemingly from nothing, it raised a few questions. Where had Ryland got his money from? And now he had been drawn into it. He had thrown in his lot with Cleadon, a man he hadn't known for very long. What was it about the old gun-fighter that evoked that kind of response? He himself hadn't used a gun in years, yet he hadn't hesitated to open fire when it seemed that to do so was the only way to stop Cleadon being lynched, even though it put his own life in danger.

Now they were both leaving town. He didn't know whether Cleadon was right or not, but he felt no regrets. There was nothing here in particular for either Cleadon or himself. Nothing. Unless maybe . . . No. Ava might miss him for a short while, but she would soon forget. He wasn't fool enough to think she would be interested in him. What was he? An ageing wrangler and horse dealer with a face like the beasts he once traded in.

He was still lost in thought when a footstep on the veranda jolted him out of his reverie. He looked up startled for a moment, but it was only Cleadon.

'Sorry,' Cleadon said. 'Didn't mean to make you jump.'

'I was just thinkin'.' Cleadon took a seat, and Cayuse handed him his bag of Bull Durham.

'What were you thinkin' about?'

'About leavin' town. Are you sure that's what you mean to do?'

'Yup. If I stay here, I shall only bring trouble.'

'From your reputation, I'd say you weren't the type to run.'

GUN LAW AT LOST BUCKET

'It's my reputation, as you call it, which has got me into this mess.'

'Sorry. I didn't mean it like it probably sounded. I know you ain't runnin'. But do you have to move on? Is it really necessary?'

'I got to admit, after what those varmints did to me, there's a part of me wants to ride straight back to the Hat R and deal with them. But that would only make things worse.'

'You mean like you did with those towns that you tamed?'

'Yes, if you want to put it that way. But in any event, that ain't the way things are done now, and not the way things should be done.'

'You still OK about me comin' with you?'

'Were you serious about that?'

'Of course. Never been more serious.'

'And you ain't changed your mind?'

'Nope. I'm ready when you are.' Cleadon blew out a widening ring of smoke.

'I guess you'll need to make a few arrangements. How about. . . .'

'Arrangements, hell!' Cayuse said. 'I live above the livery stable. My horse is right here. I don't even need to go back, though I'll just head over and tell Jud what I'm doin'.'

'The ostler?'

'Yeah. I've been doin' him a favour livin' there and helpin' out.'

He looked more closely at Cleadon.

'Are you sure you're OK though?'

'Sure. I was a bit shook up, but I'm fine. I'd have just been wastin' the doc's time even if he'd been available.' Cleadon suddenly winced and clutched at his shoulder.

'Thought you said you were OK?' Cayuse said.

'It's nothin'.' He rubbed his shoulder for a few moments.

'Anyway,' he continued, 'I was gonna say how about we meet tomorrow at sunup?'

'I don't know,' Cayuse replied. 'I'm as keen as you to get goin', but you've been through a bit of an ordeal.'

'All right,' Cleadon said. 'Give it another day. How about we ride out the day after?'

'You could maybe do with more time.'

'I'll be fine. Besides, we don't want to wait too long. The whole point is to avoid trouble with Cass Ryland. He's gonna get to hear about his son sooner rather than later. We want to be gone by the time he does.'

For a moment Cayuse looked unconvinced, but then a smile slowly spread across his features.

'The day after tomorrow,' he said. 'At sun-up.' Cleadon got to his feet.

'Just give me a minute,' he said. He came back after a few moments with a bottle and a couple of tumblers.

'I've got somethin' here that's a mite better than your darned tarantula juice; although I got to admit

26

it worked wonders this afternoon.' He poured the whiskey into the tumblers.

'What are we drinkin' to?' Cayuse asked. Cleadon shrugged.

'I ain't sure,' he said, 'but let's drink anyway.'

It was late that night when Cayuse finally took his leave of Cleadon. He was none too steady on his feet. The next day passed. Cleadon was feeling a lot better, but he wasn't sure about Cayuse. He wouldn't have been entirely surprised had the oldster not turned up at all. In the cold light of day, maybe he would think differently about simply upping sticks and leaving town. But Cayuse was true to his word, and appeared soon after the first rays of dawn had spread across the sky.

'I figure we could use some grub,' Cleadon said.

'I was hopin' you'd say that.' It didn't take long for Cleadon to throw some ham and eggs into a pan and brew some strong coffee. While they were eating, Cayuse seemed quieter than his usual self.

'You're still quite sure about this?' Cleadon asked.

'Of course I'm sure. You've no need to ask.'

'It's just that you don't seem to be sayin' much.'

'We talked it all through,' Cayuse said. 'If I seem quiet, it's probably because of my head.'

'You know that Cass Ryland is likely to come lookin' for me?'

'He's got cause to come after me too,' Cayuse

replied. 'But like I just said, we've already been through that.'

They were silent for a time. Cleadon poured a second mug of coffee for them both. Cayuse took a swig before turning to Cleadon.

'As a matter of fact,' he said, 'there is one thing that's troublin' me.'

'Yeah? And what's that?'

'Well, given what you just said about Cass Ryland, I figure I'd feel a lot more comfortable if on this occasion you would just forget about goin' unarmed, and strap on some side arms again.' Cleadon seemed to consider his words for a moment before replying.

'Funny you should say that,' he said. 'Last night, after you'd gone, I got to thinkin'.' He paused.

'Thinkin' what?' Cayuse said.

'That it wouldn't be right or fair to drag you into this without takin' precautions.'

'You didn't drag me into it,' Cayuse said. 'I volunteered.'

'OK. You volunteered. But whatever way you look at it, things could get hot, and if they do, I wouldn't expect anyone to do my fightin' for me.' A slow grin began to spread across Cayuse's features.

'So you. . . .'

Cleadon nodded.

'I've dusted down my old .44s,' he said. Cayuse let out a whoop.

'Don't get me wrong. I'm just hopin' I never have

to use 'em. But just in case. . . .'

'You might be needin' a rifle?' Cayuse said. It was Cleadon's turn to grin.

'Already packed,' he said.

'Then we're ready to go.'

'We sure are. There's just one thing. I figured it might be an idea to let the marshal know what we're doin', so I've already left him a note. If anyone else is interested, he can pass it on. Otherwise he might start mountin' a posse or somethin' and come lookin' for us.'

'Good thinkin',' Cayuse replied. For a moment the thought of Ava passed across his mind. Not that she would care. It was quickly gone.

'OK then,' Cleadon said. 'Let's ride.'

CHAPTER TWO

It was a quiet afternoon in Deerwood. Marshal Dunbar was standing on the boardwalk outside his office observing the scene. Because it was so quiet, it was the sound of approaching hoof beats that first put him on the alert. Half a dozen riders appeared, spread across the street, and at their head he recognized Cass Ryland. Even from a distance, he sensed that trouble was in the air, and he was pretty sure he knew why. They came to a halt and Ryland dismounted. His face was grim and there was thunder in his glance. He came up close to the marshal.

'What kind of a town do you run?' he snapped.

Dunbar looked beyond him to his gang of riders. They were all heavily armed.

'A peaceful town. That's why I'm going to have to ask your boys to check in their side irons. And their rifles too.'

Ryland gave him a long hard stare.

'Don't push me,' he hissed.

'You've read the ordinances. You know the score.'

'I'm not here to pussyfoot with you,' Ryland said. 'I'm here because I want some answers.'

He pushed past and crashed through the door of the marshal's office. With a second glance at the gang of riders, Dunbar followed him and slammed the door. From Cleadon's note, he knew that the old gunfighter had left town. But Cleadon hadn't made it clear what had happened out at the Hat R. It was pretty obvious from his demeanour that Ryland knew about the death of his son. Had Cleadon told him? Or had he heard about it from some other source? It wouldn't be surprising. News of what had occurred at Ava's eating house would soon have got about. Anyone could have relayed the news back to the Hat R. Maybe one of Ryland's own men had been in town. Even so, it hadn't taken very long. Any doubts he had on the matter, however, were dispelled quickly.

'I want Dane Cleadon. Where is he?'

'Dane Cleadon?'

'You know damn well who I mean. You know everyone in town. You've told me that yourself – you pride yourself on it. So where is Dane Cleadon?'

'Even if I knew who you are talking about or where he is, it wouldn't be information I could share with you.'

'I'm warnin' you, Marshal. If I have to tear this

31

whole town apart, I aim to find Cleadon. Tell me where he is. You'll be savin' yourself a whole heap of trouble.'

'Don't threaten me,' Dunbar replied. 'You may be the biggest noise round these parts, but you ain't above the law.'

Ryland gave the marshal a long, hard stare and then made for the door.

'I tried to give you a chance,' he stormed. 'Since you refuse to cooperate, you can face the consequences.'

It was the rancher's turn to slam the door. As the room still reverberated with the noise, Dunbar opened it once more. Ryland was just climbing into leather.

'Don't do anything foolish!' he shouted.

Ryland raised himself in the stirrups and took a look all around.

'You ain't no kind of a marshal!' he yelled back. 'If you were, you wouldn't be shelterin' no criminal. You had your chance. Now you can take what's comin'.'

Without further ado, he dug his spurs into the horse's flanks and began to ride away. The other riders quickly followed. The marshal watched them till they turned a corner, and then went back inside. He was uncertain what he should do next. What did Ryland intend doing? Apart from the fact that his men were all carrying firearms, they had broken no law. Still, they were clearly looking for trouble.

Something was about to explode, and he needed to be ready for it when it did.

Cleadon and Cayuse rode at a slow pace. For the present at least, they were not aiming for anywhere in particular. Their sole intention was to put some ground between themselves and Deerwood. It was a fine day, and they both felt good. Cleadon's bruises caused him some pain and his injured shoulder felt stiff, but otherwise he seemed to have made a good recovery.

'There must definitely be something in that medicine of yours,' he remarked.

'Never fails,' Cayuse replied. 'Only thing that ever equalled that concoction is this.'

He reached into the pocket of his jacket and produced what looked like a stone.

'Ain't any normal kind of stone,' Cayuse said. 'Got it from the insides of a cow. If any of those cuts of yours got infected, this would draw it all out, like as not. Works best when it's soaked in milk.'

He handed it to Cleadon who looked at it suspiciously. He weighed it in his hand.

'Whatever you say,' he replied.

'People think they know things,' Cayuse said. 'Me, I say there's lots of things we don't know about. You ever read the Bard?'

'The Bard?'

'Shakespeare. There's somethin' in there that somebody says. Can't quite recall it. Somethin'

33

about there bein' more things than folk give credit for. I got some theories. I'll tell you about 'em sometime.'

'I'll look forward to it,' Cleadon replied.

'I used to do a mite of readin'. Still do. In the early days it was mainly catalogues and farm journals. Sometimes there'd be a few yeller-back novels lyin' about the bunkhouse. Then one time, some drummer came along sellin' encyclopaedies. It was leafin' through those old tomes that really got me goin'. I used to carry some readin' matter in my saddle-bags.'

'Used to? Not any more?'

'Nope. Maybe I should. I once knew a man got shot and was saved because the bullet lodged in an old Bible he carried in his jacket.'

'They say the Bible saves,' Cleadon commented.

'I don't think that's quite what they had in mind,' Cayuse replied.

They lapsed into silence, each thinking his own thoughts. Cleadon took to observing the country through which they were travelling more closely. It was an old habit. In the days when so often he had had to rely on his wits and his gun, it paid to be very familiar with his surroundings. It was a fine, open but rather flat landscape, with stands of willow and aspen in the water courses and an occasional prairie dog town. There was no indication as yet of the high country towards which they were heading.

'Remind me how far till we get to the hills?'

Cleadon asked.

'About another three days' ride, I reckon.'

Cayuse knew the locale better than Cleadon, but there had been little choice as to which way they went. West and south of town was Hat R territory. To the south the land ran into scrub and semi-desert. So they were heading east. For the time being and until they decided otherwise. In point of fact, Cleadon had another reason for opting to go in that direction. Among the hills, he had a better chance of eluding Cass Ryland, whom he had no doubts would sooner or later be on their trail.

Marshal Dunbar was uneasy. He hadn't seen nor heard anything of Cass Ryland and his boys since he had watched them ride out of sight. He had done the rounds of the town, calling in at the saloons, but there was no sign of them. They seemed to have vanished from sight. People had seen them – they would have been hard to miss – but they were nowhere around. Yet the marshal felt sure they were somewhere in the vicinity. He was confident that they had not returned to the Hat R. Cass Ryland's state of mind was sufficient guarantee that he wouldn't be content to lie easy. He had made it perfectly clear that he meant to find Dane Cleadon, and the threat he had thrown out was all the more menacing in being vague.

He tried to focus his attention on the paperwork he had in hand, but couldn't concentrate, and kept

getting to his feet to go outside and pace up and
down the boardwalk. There was nothing out of the
ordinary in prospect. Folk passed, going about their
business. An occasional horseman rode by. A buckboard drew up outside the main emporium. A dog
lifted its leg to urinate against a stanchion. As he
walked, he lifted his hat to people that he knew.
There was nothing to differentiate the day from any
other day, but somehow he felt apprehensive.
Something intangible seemed to hang in the air.
Maybe, he thought, it was his own nerves. The
sudden incursion of Ryland and his men had unsettled him. Maybe a drink would help his nerves calm
down. He began to make his way towards the saloon
when suddenly he was stopped in his tracks by the
sight of a thin column of smoke rising into the air
from somewhere towards the edge of town.

'What the hell is that?' someone shouted. The
cloud grew and thickened, and sparks began to
shoot into the air.

'Somethin' on fire!' Dunbar called.

There were sounds of running feet. The saloon
batwings flew open and people spilled out, looking
around in confusion. Over the tops of the false-
fronted buildings, flames began to shoot into the
sky. Struggling to gather his wits, the marshal began
to run in the direction of the smoke and flames. As
he tore along, his brain registered what had happened, but only as he rounded a corner and saw
that the burning building ahead of him was

Cleadon's cabin did he make the connection with what had happened earlier.

'Ryland!' he hissed.

He had been right to feel anxious. His instincts had not lied. Right in front of him was the first instalment of Ryland's revenge.

He came to a halt as thick smoke came billowing towards him. Some of the other townsfolk were arriving on the scene, coughing and spluttering as the noxious fumes entered their throats and lungs. Some of the more enterprising among them were already attempting to dowse the fire by pouring buckets of water on the leaping flames. A few others were beating at the flames with blankets. The marshal took off his bandana, fastened it over the lower half of his face and then hurried to join the fire-fighters. He took his place in a line of people forming a human chain passing buckets of water along. Soon they were joined by more helpers as people rallied to the cause. As he worked to contain the fire, he reflected that it was just as well that Cleadon's shack was in an isolated position on the edge of town. If not, the flames would have quickly spread and the whole town might have been engulfed. He was certain that Ryland and his boys were behind it. Would Ryland have cared if the entire town had been set ablaze? As it was, the danger still existed and it was only the efforts of the townsfolk which in the end prevented the fire from spreading. The nearest building was dowsed with water and people were beating out the sparks and embers landing on the ground between, which threatened to spread the blaze.

He had no time to pursue his thoughts. The fire was still raging and the heat was intense. He heard the sound of wheels above the crackle of the flames. A buckboard lumbered into view. It was carrying barrels of water and people began to hand them down and haul them to where the fire was at its most intense. Some of the people wielding sheets and blankets soaked them in the water. Everyone was working furiously, but the struggle was in the balance. Even with the arrival of the buckboard, there was barely enough water for the job in hand.

As they all toiled and laboured to put out the blaze, the fierce heat scorched their faces and arms and blackened their features. Dunbar's bandana did little to protect him. His eyes burned and stung, and his lungs felt as though they were seared. He took a moment to look around. It seemed to him that the blaze was beginning to dwindle, and it was soon clear that it had been contained. But there seemed to be little point in trying to save any remnant of Cleadon's shack.

As if other people had reached the same conclusion, they began to slow down and back away, allowing the rest of the fire to burn itself out. They staggered back to watch the flames consume the cabin and begin to die away. No one spoke. They were exhausted. They had been in a battle. In a sense they had won. The fire had been contained. The destruction, though complete, was limited in scope. Somehow, though, it seemed a pyrrhic victory.

'I guess that's about it, folks,' the marshal called. 'Thanks to everyone for helping to put this fire out and stopping it spread.'

'What do you think happened?' someone asked. 'How do you figure that fire got started in the first place?'

The marshal shook his head. He knew the answer to the question, but he wasn't going to start that hare running. As the last traces of Cleadon's shack crumbled into a mass of glowing embers, the people began to disperse. The marshal stood a while longer before beginning to make his way towards his own house. When he reached it, the first thing he did was to pour himself a stiff drink. In the light of what had happened, he needed to puzzle out what his response should be. He had no doubts that Ryland was responsible for the blaze. It was obvious that the rancher knew about the death of his son, and the torching of Cleadon's shack was his first response.

Would he be content to leave it at that? None of it was the town's affair, but in his blind rage would Ryland see it that way? Cleadon had left in order to avoid trouble for anyone else, but had he miscalculated?

*

39

Cleadon and Cayuse rode steadily the rest of the day, stopping at regular intervals to save their horses. Towards evening they reached a creek with undercut banks which made a good site to set up camp for the night. They stripped the gear from the horses and gave them a chance to roll before watering and feeding them. They built a fire, put slabs of meat in the skillet, and as the kettle of water began to boil, dropped in the coffee. Neither of them spoke much. It was cool and still. Only the crackle of the fire broke the quiet as their horses cropped contentedly on the sparse grass. As they ate, darkness descended and the shy stars began to emerge. When they had finished their meal, they rolled cigarettes and lay back, resting their heads on their saddles.

'Sure is peaceful,' Cayuse remarked.

'I guess I've kinda missed nights like this,' Cleadon replied.

'Yeah. Livin' in town . . . I don't know. It makes a man forget.'

'Forget what?'

'I ain't sure. But somethin' important.'

Cayuse paused to take a long sup of coffee.

'Maybe I'm gettin' maudlin,' he concluded.

'Maybe we're just gettin' old,' Cleadon replied.

'Times sure have changed. And not always for the best.'

'I don't know about that. Life was pretty rough and ready in the old days. Things have settled

40

down. People's lives are better. More secure. The country's grown up.'

'If so, then it's down to people like you.'

Cleadon took a drag on his cigarette before replying.

'I don't know about that. I'm not proud of what I did. Maybe there wasn't much to choose between me and all those others who made a livin' by the gun.'

'You were on the right side, the side of law and order. Those others – they deserved everythin' they got. The world's a better place without them.'

'Who knows? Under different circumstances, maybe the roles would have been reversed. Maybe it would have been me ridin' the owlhoot trail.'

'There was no chance of that. Not with you. With me it might have been the case.'

'Why do you say that?'

'There've been times when I took a wrong turn. Hell, it might have been me on the other side from you.'

Cleadon poured them both another mug of coffee.

'How did you come by your name?' he asked. 'I take it Cayuse ain't the name you were born with.'

'I've been around horses so much I guess I've grown to look like one. I used to help run a horse ranch. I was wrangler for a few outfits. Some of them were a mite 'ornery, I can tell you.'

'But not like the Hat R?'

41

Cayuse grunted.

'Nope. From the way you were treated, I'd say Cass Ryland is in a class of his own.'

Cleadon turned to him.

'You know they'll be comin' after us?'

'We've been over that.'

'And you know what we can expect if we fall into Ryland's hands?'

Cayuse blew out a smoke ring.

'Sure. Then I guess we'd better not let that happen.'

Ava Feld was just setting out the tables in her eating house when the door was flung open and three men came in. Two of them sat at one table and the third at another. They put their legs up so that their spurs raked the chairs.

'No offence,' Ava said, 'but would you mind putting your feet down?'

The two sitting together exchanged glances while the third looked at her through cold eyes.

'Three beers,' he said.

'I'm afraid we don't serve alcohol. I could get you some coffee. But can you take your feet off the chairs first please?'

'My name is Seb,' he retorted. 'What's yours?'

'That's really none of your business.'

'Now that ain't bein' friendly,' he replied.

He continued to stare at her, but then suddenly he kicked the chair on which his feet were resting aside and stood up. With a quick move, he grabbed hold of her by the waist and drew her to him.

'I've taken my feet off the chair,' he said. 'Now how about showin' me a little gratitude?'

She struggled to free herself but he held her in an iron grip. Putting his other hand behind her head, he forced his face towards his. The other two were laughing and shouting encouragement to their companion. She tried hard to evade his grasp but it was no use. As he pressed his lips on hers the only thing she could do was to bite him on the lip. Instantly he recoiled. He put his hand to his bleeding lip and then struck her hard on her cheek. She staggered backwards, but before she could do anything he had seized her again and was pressing her against a wall. Ignoring her struggles and her protests, he reached down and began to tug at her skirts. The others were about to join him when he suddenly seemed to lose interest. Letting her go, he stood back before striking her again with the back of his hand.

'You ain't worth it, you ugly bitch,' he snarled.

He looked around at the eating house before turning back to her.

'Nice place,' he said. 'Pity it's goin' out of business.'

He nodded to the others, and with a whoop and a yell they started to smash the place up. It didn't take long till it was a complete shambles. Still clutching at her torn garments, Ava could only look on in fear and bewilderment. When they had finished the man called Seb turned to her again.

'You know someone called Dane Cleadon. Well, that was your mistake.'

He looked at her as if he was about to strike her again, but instead he began to move away. As the three intruders stood in the doorway, one of them added:

'If you see Cleadon again, you can tell him from us that he's a dead man.'

'But then again,' the one called Seb added, 'I figure it just wouldn't be healthy to have anythin' to do with him.'

He spat on the floor. Chortling with laughter, they went out, slamming the door behind them. Ava sank to the floor amid the wreckage of her eating house. She was bleeding from the nose and lips and the taste of blood was in her mouth. She needed help, and it didn't take long for it to arrive – just long enough for her attackers to have mounted their horses and ridden from view. Someone sent for the doctor and the marshal, and they arrived more or less together. Between them, they helped her upstairs to her rooms above the eating house where she lay on a chaise longue as the doctor attended her.

'You've got a nasty cut to your mouth and damage to your nose, but I don't think it's broken.'

'It hurts,' she replied.

'You're likely to have a couple of black eyes by

44

tomorrow,' the doctor replied. He dug in his briefcase and produced some tablets.

'These should help with the pain,' he said. He looked at the marshal.

'Who would do something like this?' he asked. Dunbar shook his head.

'In all my time as marshal,' he replied, 'I can't recall ever seeing something like this.' He turned to Ava,

'What happened?' he asked.

'I don't know. There were three men. . . .'

'Did you recognize them?'

'No, I'm afraid not.' She thought for a moment. 'But I know the name of the man who beat me. One of the others called him by name. It was Seb.'

The marshal considered for a moment, as if he was trying to remember something.

'It's a pretty common name,' he concluded. 'Still, it's useful to know.'

'Whoever it was, they caused an awful lot of damage,' the doctor said. 'I mean to the property.'

'They sure have,' the marshal said. He turned to Ava.

'Can you think of any reason why somebody would want to trash the place? Has anyone got a grudge against you?'

Ava shook her head.

'I think Miss Feld could do with some rest,' the doctor said. 'Maybe that's enough questions for now.'

'Yeah. Of course.' He began to make for the door.

'Don't worry about the mess,' he said. 'I'll see that it gets cleaned up pronto. And if you think of anything, be sure to let me know.' Together with the doctor, he made his way back down the stairs.

'It's a terrible thing,' the doctor said. 'A terrible thing. For the life of me, I can't understand why anyone would do that to a lady.'

'You're right, it is a terrible thing,' the marshal replied. 'It makes it even worse that we've both known Ava for a long time. But I aim to make sure that whoever is responsible pays the full penalty of the law.'

They walked part of the way down the street together before separating. The marshal was turning things over in his mind. He knew more than he was prepared to let the doctor know. First Cleadon's cabin had been burned down. Now Ava's eating house had been wrecked. It was on her premises that Tim Ryland had met his end. It didn't take a lot of thought to figure out that Cass Ryland was behind both events. To make it even more certain, he had just remembered where he had heard the name Seb before. A man called Seb Leitch was the foreman of the Hat R. His course of action was becoming clear. He needed to pay Ryland a visit.

The lights were burning late that night at the Hat R. At least the boys in the bunkhouse were enjoying themselves. Cass Ryland, sensing their high spirits, had given them leave to celebrate. He himself sat alone and disconsolate in the isolation of his study in the ranch-house, set some distance apart from the other buildings. A glass of whiskey and a half-empty bottle stood at his elbow, but drinking had done little to dull his senses. The noise coming from the bunkhouse was faint and muffled. He could barely hear it above the regular ticking of a clock on the mantelpiece. The lamp was turned low. A thin wisp of smoke rose into the air from a cigar he had lit and then laid aside. The acrid smell of fire from Cleadon's burning cabin still seemed to linger in his nostrils. Despite himself, he was beginning to feel drowsy when there was a rap on the door that brought him instantly alert.

'Come in!' he called.

The door opened and a lank figure with a sallow expression and straggling hair stepped into the room.

'Ah, Leitch,' Ryman said, 'I was expecting you.' He gestured towards a cabinet. 'Fetch yourself a glass.'

The man did so and then sat opposite Ryland, who poured them both a stiff drink. They each took a swig.

'The boys have been lettin' off steam,' Ryland continued. 'That's fine, I'm sure you've got it all under control. But I take it the ones you've picked will be ready to ride with us tomorrow?'

The man's features registered some surprise.

'You're comin' too?' he said.

'Of course. What did you expect? This place more or less runs itself -- thanks to your input, of course. Teller can take care of things while we're gone. I take it you've introduced your man to the others?'

'Yeah. He's fittin' in.'

'He doesn't have to fit in. Just so long as he leads us to that murderin' scum Dane Cleadon.'

'Don't you worry about that, he's one of the best trackers in the business.'

'You can vouch for him?'

'I fought with him against the Sioux and the Cheyenne. He's part Indian himself.'

'Good. I know I can rely on you, Seb.'

'You're quite sure Cleadon has left town?'

'I have it on good report. He was seen heading out of town with another man. From my sources, I gather he's an oldster who goes by the name of Cayuse.'

Leitch laughed hoarsely.

'Two old timers. This should be easy.'

'Just remember, I want Cleadon taken alive. A bullet is too good for him. I've got other plans in mind.'

Leitch chortled again.

'I sure wouldn't like to be in his shoes when we catch up with him,' he said.

He paused for a moment, as if struck by a sudden thought.

'It's funny,' he said, 'but me and a few of the boys were out ridin' and we came across some dude trespassin' on Hat R property.'

Ryland showed interest.

'When was this?' he asked.

'Day before yesterday.'

'I take it you took the appropriate measures to discourage him?'

'Yeah, we sure did.'

'Then what's the issue?'

'Nothin' really. It's just that he said he wanted to see you. I didn't think anything of it at the time. But it seems a bit odd, lookin' back.'

Ryland considered his words.

'What, you think it might have some bearing on . . . It wasn't the marshal, was it?'

'Nope, not the marshal. Probably nobody in particular.'

'It certainly wouldn't have been Cleadon, if that's what you're thinkin'. He'd be the last person to come riding this way. In fact we've already seen what his reaction is – to run away with his tail between his legs like a low-down polecat.'

'I guess you're right. Well, whoever he was, he won't be back again.' Leitch looked at his empty glass, but when it became clear that Ryland wasn't about to offer him another, he got to his feet.

'Reckon I'll be turnin' in,' he said.

'Yeah. Me too. We got some hard ridin' to do startin' tomorrow.'

Leitch slouched across the room and out the door. Ryland remained seated for a while before eventually standing up and following his foreman outside. He paused on the veranda. The sounds from the bunkhouse had finally dwindled. Down in one of the corrals a horse whinnied. Otherwise the night was silent. He gazed into the wide empty spaces. Somewhere out there was the man who had killed his son. He meant to hunt him down and have his revenge.

Before setting out for the Hat R, Marshal Dunbar paid a call on Ava. The windows of the wrecked eating house had been boarded up and the debris inside cleared away. He went up the stairs, and when he knocked on the door it was answered almost immediately. He wasn't surprised to see Ava up and about, but he still asked the obligatory question.

'Shouldn't you be lyin' down and takin' it easy?'

She shook her head.

'I'm feeling a bit sore, but I'm OK. I mean to open up later.'

'That would probably be pushin' it.'

'I'm in business. I can't afford to be taking time out.'

'Shouldn't you wait and see what the doctor says?'

Her face was puffy and bruised and her lip swollen. It wasn't possible to tell what other damage she had suffered.

'The doctor's done his bit,' she replied. 'The way I figure it, the quickest way to mend is to keep busy.'

Dunbar grinned.

'Well, I guess you know what's best.' He turned to go.

'Won't you stay for a cup of coffee? Or maybe something a little stronger?'

'I'd like to, but I've got some business myself that needs attendin' to.'

'Are you sure?'

'How about if I stop by later? I could lend a hand if you need some assistance.'

'That would be nice.'

He looked at her closely.

'Just don't go overdoin' things,' he said.

He went back down the stairs and through the eating house, closing the outside door carefully behind him. The street was coming to life as he made his way to the livery where his horse was stabled. He quickly saddled the roan and led it outside where he stepped into leather. Once he had passed out of town he broke into a canter. He was feeling apprehensive, but the cool morning air and the rhythmic beat of his horse's hoofs served to steady him. If he had had any illusions concerning the sort of man he had to deal with in Cass Ryland, recent events had served to set him straight. Apart from any other consideration, however, he had the authority of his badge to support him. He meant to take Seb Leitch under arrest and take him back for questioning. Whether Ryland would comply with the arrest of his foreman was a debatable issue.

As he neared the Hat R ranch-house, he was on the alert for any signs of trouble. He was only too aware of what had happened to Dane Cleadon. When the ranch-house came into view, however, he was struck by the general air of desertion that hung about the place. He rode into the yard, stepped down from the saddle and knocked on the door. He waited a while and then knocked again. There was no reply. He rattled the handle but the door was locked. He looked through the windows; there was nobody inside. Stepping down off the veranda, he made his way across the yard and finally saw someone seated on the top bar of the corral. The corral was empty.

'Howdy,' he said, coming up.

The man returned his greeting but otherwise showed no interest.

'I'm lookin' for Cass Ryland,' the marshal said.

'What about?'

'That's between him and me.'

The man seemed to ponder this reply for a moment before gathering a mouthful of sputum and aiming it in a perfect arc towards a fence post.

'Then it looks like you've come here for nothin',' the man replied.

'Nothin'? How's that?'

'Because Mr Ryland and some of the boys left

earlier this mornin'.'

Dunbar looked around.

'How many of them?' he asked.

'I dunno. Mr Ryland doesn't tell me his business. He left me in charge, though.'

'Looks like you're doin' a good job,' Dunbar said. 'I don't suppose you have any idea where they were headed?'

The man shrugged.

'Like I say. . . .'

'I know. Ryland doesn't tell you his business. Well, thanks for the information. It's been nice to meet you. What's your name, by the way?'

'Teller. Not that I see it's of any interest to you.'

'I'm the law round these parts,' Dunbar replied. 'Lots of things are of interest to me.' He paused for a second. 'Is Seb anywhere around?'

'Seb? Nope. I figure he must have rode out with Mr Ryland.'

Dunbar turned on his heels. As he walked away, Teller's reedy voice rang out behind him.

'Is there a message you'd like me to give Mr Ryland? I mean, if he should come back any time soon.'

'No message,' Dunbar replied.

He walked back to where the roan was tethered to the hitch-rack, climbed into the saddle, and with a final glance around, rode away. He thought about what Teller had told him. There had been no sign of Ryland and his gang in town, and he hadn't passed them on his way to the ranch, but they could only be bent on more trouble. It was a fair bet that they were going after Cleadon and Cayuse. All the same, he spurred his horse and rode fairly hard, worried about what he might find when he got back.

As he rode down the main drag, he breathed a sigh of relief. Things seemed to be entirely normal. After what Ryland had done to Cleadon's cabin and what his men had done to Ava, he wouldn't put anything past Ryland. The town was still in one piece and his deputy hadn't anything to report. That probably meant his supposition that Ryland and his gang of desperados were on the trail of Cleadon was probably correct. He knew something of Cleadon's previous reputation and he reckoned that, despite their years, Cleadon and Cayuse could make a fair job of looking after themselves in normal circumstances. However, things were far from normal. All in all, he didn't rate their chances.

CHAPTER THREE

Cayuse was right about how long it would take them to reach the hills. After three days he and Cleadon were riding the high country.

'Maybe you told me what we're doin' here,' Cayuse said, 'but if so I've forgotten.'

'Not too sure myself,' Cleadon replied.

'We could have kept ridin' east and carried on till we reached the next town. We could have made for the railroad and got clean away.'

'I thought about doin' it,' Cleadon replied. 'In fact, that was my original plan, in so far as I had one. Just keep goin'.'

'What made you change your mind?'

'I haven't exactly changed it.'

'Seems thataway.'

'Maybe. The way I figure things, I'm thinkin' it might be worth checkin' out the situation with Ryland.'

'What? We both know what the situation is.

Ryland is comin' to get us. The only sensible plan is to stay ahead of him.'

'We can do that. But it might not be a bad idea to see exactly what we're up against. We don't know for sure that Ryland's comin'. We don't know how many of his boys he'll be bringin' along with him. I figure it's just as well to know those sorts of things.'

'You're thinkin' back to the War again.'

'Didn't do me no harm. I'm here, ain't I?'

Cayuse chuckled.

'I guess it wouldn't hurt,' he said. 'In any event, Ryland can't be too far behind. What difference would it make to hang around and let him get even closer?'

His irony was not lost on Cleadon.

'Let's carry on higher into the hills', he said, 'until we find a spot where we can see clearly. We should be able to spot a fly on a mule's backside from up here, never mind Ryland and whoever he's got ridin' for him.'

'Maybe we're mistaken. Maybe he won't come this way.'

'You don't believe that.'

'Nope. Just tryin' to reassure myself.'

'You don't need to do that either, or you wouldn't be here.' Cayuse grinned broadly. He raised himself in his stirrups and took a long look around, breathing deeply as he did so.

'Sure is nice,' he said. 'You know, I ain't enjoyed myself so much in years!'

Cleadon followed suit. Below them the trail wound its way back towards the plains, while up ahead it led through groves of trees and outcrops of rock towards a rugged escarpment over which clouds drifted in a clear blue sky. The air smelt of a tangy aromatic freshness quite different from the atmosphere of the plains.

'All this fresh air is makin' me kinda hungry,' he said.

Cayuse nodded.

'We could make camp right here,' he replied.

'It's temptin', but the horses will be needin' a drink soon. We got a couple of hours ridin' yet before it starts gettin' dark. Let's carry on a little further till we find a spring.'

They rode on, climbing steadily all the while. Their mounts were sure-footed but at no point was the trail too steep. At times they saw evidence that prospectors had been there: an old can, a battered tin bucket, and at one point, a rusted pickaxe. They crossed a number of dry washes and stream beds where only a trickle of water remained till they reached a creek where the water flowed freely, sparkling in the declining sun. Nearby was a dead-fall, a tree that had toppled over. They dismounted and let the horses drink while they replenished their canteens. Cayuse looked wistfully at the stream.

'Maybe we should do some pannin' for gold,' he said.

'Have you ever tried it?'

'Nope. Not sure how I'd begin.'

'I did once. If you ask me, it's a fool's game.'

'By all accounts, some folk did pretty well up here.'

'I'd be willin' to bet that an awful lot more didn't.'

'There was quite a stir at one time. It's one reason Blue Bluff got goin', providin' supplies and all. But it didn't last.'

'Why was that?'

'I don't know. There were rumours of some sort of trouble. More likely the gold just ran out.'

'Yeah. I guess that's the way of things.'

Cayuse looked about him.

'I've heard tell there's an old settlement somewhere up in these hills. A kinda ghost town. Maybe we'll come across it.'

'The hills cover a lot of territory.'

'I guess if there is an old town, it can't ever have amounted to much.'

'More likely some old mining camp.'

'Maybe there's still some gold waitin' to be found out there,' Cayuse said. Cleadon didn't reply, but instead walked over to a clump of boulders where, for a few moments, he vanished before reappearing astride a flat-topped rock. He looked out over the panorama below him and then signalled for Cayuse to join him.

'What do you reckon?' he said. 'It's a pretty good

view from here. We don't need to climb any higher.'

'I think you're right.'

'We've got good cover and plenty of water on hand. I figure we might as well set up camp right here and make it our vantage point.'

'Like you, I'm gettin' kinda hungry,' Cayuse replied. 'I'm all for makin' ourselves at home and gettin' some of that bacon and beans in the skillet.'

After they had attended to the horses, it didn't take them long to get a fire started, using some branches from the deadfall together with a few slabs of bark. Darkness was already gathering in the valley below. A breeze began to blow from the higher slopes, but by the time the evening drew down the meal was ready and they were settled and comfortable.

'There's just one thing worryin' me some,' Cayuse remarked between mouthfuls of food.

'Only one thing?'

'I've taken a shine to this style of livin', but ain't we gonna run out of supplies at some point?'

'I wouldn't worry too much about that. I figure we can always live off the land if necessary.'

Cayuse took a swig of coffee and immediately spat it out again.

'Ouch!' he said. 'Burned my mouth.'

Cleadon laughed. 'If that's the worst thing that happens, you'll be a lucky man,' he said. He reached out and threw a few more branches on the fire. Sparks leaped and danced. The wind had decreased and the night was very still. Above them the stars gleamed and glittered.

'Kinda puts things in perspective, don't it?' Cayuse remarked.

'What does?'

'The night. The quiet. Seems to me folk spend too much time fussin' and fightin'. Maybe they'd look at things differently if they spent a few nights like this up in the hills.'

When they had finished eating, Cleadon took out his pouch of tobacco, took what he needed and handed it to Cayuse. They both lit up.

'Things turn out differently from what you expect, don't you think?' Cleadon remarked.

'You mean us bein' here and on the run?' Cayuse replied.

'Yeah, but not just that. You know, at one time I wanted to be a lawyer. It didn't work out that way. But when I was a boy, I used to sneak into the general store and listen to the old men gabbin'. As often as not the talk was about some trial that had taken place. That and politics. They never seemed to mind me hangin' around, but if for any reason I didn't go inside, I would sit on the sidewalk and listen to them talkin' while I played jacks. That's how I got the idea of becomin' a lawyer. But like I said, things didn't work out that way.'

'You sound regretful.'

'Maybe a little bit, but it don't get you anywhere.' He took a long drag at his cigarette.

'What about you, Cayuse?' he asked. 'Did you ever have ambitions to be anythin'?'

Cayuse scratched his chin.

'I once had the idea of bein' a writer. I used to spend time when I was a boy around the local news-paper offices. I got to do odd jobs, but the paper went out of business and I never got any further.'

'Maybe you should have tried settin' up a news-paper of your own.'

Cayuse laughed.

'Perhaps,' he said, 'but readin's as far as I ever got.'

'Like those old yeller-backed novels and ency-clopaedias you were tellin' me about.'

'Yeah, that's it.'

They both fell silent, lost for a time in their own memories. Finally, Cleadon looked across at his companion.

'I guess we're both a bit too old to start anythin' now,' he quipped. Suddenly he laughed.

'Hell,' he said, 'we're gettin' kinda maudlin again. We're still here, after all, and we ain't done yet. Right now I figure it's time we turned in and got some shuteye. Who knows what we might be up against tomorrow.'

Nobody knew the tracker's name. Because he was mainly Crow Indian, he was known as Crow Jack, but most of the time it was shortened simply to Crow. He had joined the Army as a scout in the

61

battles against the Sioux, not because of any traditional enmity, but because of the money on offer. He was a good scout, however, and Cass Ryland felt that, on the whole, Leitch had done well to hire him. His own slight doubt was whether Crow was entirely trustworthy. Since none of the other six men he had brought along with him had any skills in tracking, he had no way of knowing whether Crow might just be leading them on. He had little choice in the matter.

His misgivings began to gain in strength when they approached the hills. Why would Cleadon and his companion have chosen to go in that direction? Wouldn't it have been simpler for them just to keep on riding? They could have made for a town on the railroad and got clear away. Not that that would have done them any good. He would have followed anyway. But he wasn't sure it made sense for them to choose that option. With these thoughts in mind, he drew up alongside Leitch.

'What do you reckon?' he asked. 'Do you think Cleadon would have come this way?'

'What reason would there be to think otherwise?'

'No particular reason. But ask yourself: would you have chosen to make for the hills?'

'I don't see why not.'

'You don't see it? Cleadon could have put a lot more distance between us if he'd headed for a railroad junction. Or just kept right on goin'.'

Leitch thought for a moment.

62

'What?' he concluded. 'You figure Crow is leadin' us on a wild goose chase?'

'The thought had crossed my mind.' The foreman considered the matter further.

'Nope, I don't figure he'd do that. What reason would he have?'

'Money of course. The longer he keeps us on the trail, the richer he gets.'

'I don't think he operates that way. Remember, I knew him in the wars. He built up a good reputation.'

'How well did you know him?'

'Well enough.'

'How come you got in contact with him so quickly?'

'He lives right there in Deerwood. Keeps himself to himself, but he's known around town.' Leitch paused for a moment, then said: 'Are you sure there ain't somethin' else botherin' you?'

'What do you mean?' Ryland snapped. 'What are you getting at?'

'Simmer down,' Leitch replied. 'No need to get so agitated.'

'You'd better watch what you say,' Ryland said. 'You ain't indispensable.' An ugly leer spread across the foreman's face.

'Oh,' he replied. 'I think you and I know that just ain't true. We're in it together, right up to the hilt.'

'In what together? What are you implyin'?'

'You know how things stand as well as me. Goin'

back to those hills is the last thing we want after what happened up there, but if Cleadon is headed that way, we ain't got no choice. Unless you want to abandon the whole thing.'

'I ain't abandoning anything. Just keep your opinions to yourselves and be damned sure that Indian ain't leadin' us up the garden path.'

They lapsed into an awkward silence for a while till Leitch spoke in a slightly different tone.

'Just as a matter of opinion, it seems to me like you're assumin' Cleadon and his *compadre* are plannin' to escape, to get as far away from Deerwood as they can. Could be that's the case. But have you considered that maybe they're just takin' time out and are fully intendin' comin' back again at some point? That might be why they're aimin' for the hills.'

'I don't see it that way.'

'Maybe they were just plannin' to let things simmer down for a whiles after. . . .' He didn't conclude the sentence.

'A bit late for that, if it's what they were considerin',' Ryland broke in. Leitch didn't respond, and since both reckoned they had reached the end of the conversation, they spurred their horses in order to rejoin the rest of the riders who had moved a little way ahead, with Crow Jack's skewbald paint in the lead.

The Indian was looking ahead towards the peaks. He had no doubts in his mind that their quarry had taken to the hills. To him the trail was obvious. He had no problems isolating the sign made by Cleadon and Cayuse. He could have made a fair guess as to what sort of horses they were riding, and what condition they were in. He knew what provisions they were carrying from the remains of the first camp fire they had made, despite their best efforts to conceal it. He knew why Ryland had taken him on, but his instincts told him that Ryland was not at ease about the way the pursuit had led them to where they now found themselves. Was there a reason? He would stay alert and make up his mind about his own role in the affair when the time came.

Marshal Dunbar sat in his office looking at a Wanted poster. It was old and the portrait was a poor one, but nevertheless he felt sure there was something of a resemblance to Seb Leitch. He hadn't seen Leitch in some time so that was another reason for uncertainty, but in addition to the faded picture there was a brief description that seemed to back up his hunch: *About 30 years of age; height five feet, nine inches; weight 185 pounds; dark complexion; peculiar nose, flattened at bridge; projecting brow.* It wasn't much to go on, but it fitted – especially the bit about the nose and the brow. How had he not made the connection before?

Although some stories had been circulating about Cass Ryland and the Hat R, he had not had any real reason up till now to suspect the outfit of going beyond the boundaries of the law. But the way they had treated Cleadon, and then their subsequent actions in burning down Cleadon's cabin and terrorizing Ava had caused him to think differently. That was the reason he had dug out the old Wanted poster. Everything that had happened was further cause for him to identify the man concerned with Seb Leitch. It all hung together. If it was the same man, then he had been responsible for an attempted bank robbery in South Dakota. Had he been involved in other crimes?

Suddenly a new thought struck the marshal. Leitch, if it was him, hadn't been the only person involved. Had he known Cass Ryland in those days? Cass Ryland owned the biggest spread in the territory. Where had he got the money for that? Could it have been through robbery? A whole train of thoughts had been loosed in Dunbar's head. When he wanted to think, he liked to take a walk. Getting to his feet, he placed the Wanted poster back in a drawer of his desk, put on his hat and stepped out into the daylight.

The street was busy. He paused for a moment to let a buckboard pass and then bent his steps in the direction of Ava's eating house. He hadn't intended doing so, but as he walked he suddenly began to feel hungry. When he opened the door and stepped inside he was pleased to see that the place had been restored to its former condition. No one would have realized that the place had been trashed not long before. Ava herself was sitting at one of the tables but immediately rose to her feet.

'It's good to see you, Marshal,' she said.

'Good to see you, too. How are you feelin?'

'Right as rain again. Well, maybe not quite, but I'm sure gettin' there.' The marshal glanced around. A few customers sat at the tables and there was a faint murmur of conversation.

'Take a seat,' Ava said. She moved away as he did so, and came back with a glass and a bottle of beer.

'Have this for the time being,' she said. 'And anything you might want, it's on the house.'

'I couldn't let you do that. You've got a livin' to make the same as the rest of us.'

'After what you did for me, it's the least I can do.'

He was about to argue the point but she held up her hand to stop him. He grinned.

'What have you got then?' he asked.

She drew his attention to a menu that stood on the table. He picked it up. The items were listed under separate headings for breakfast, dinner and supper, and there was a range of items.

'This is new,' he said.

'I figured the place needed an upgrade. I've taken on a girl to help with the cooking. I'm even thinkin' about moving to new premises, bigger premises. I've got plans,' she replied.

Dunbar looked at her. Either she was putting on a brave front or she had put her bad experience at

67

the hands of Seb Leitch behind her.

'I can especially recommend the roast pork,' she said. He looked at the menu: roast pork with dressing, mashed potatoes, gravy, pickles, white and graham bread, cheese and coffee.

'Sounds mighty good to me,' he said.

'Comin' right up,' she replied.

She left him to go into the kitchen. He drank some of the beer and glanced out of the window. Things seemed peaceful enough. The attack on the restaurant and the burning of Cleadon's shack might never have happened. But they had happened, and it was his duty to see that they didn't happen again. Outbreaks of trouble were inevitable, but they had to be kept to a minimum. Musing that way, he had a sudden thought. It meant asking Ava about Ryland. He would have hesitated to do so had she not already referred in passing to the incident with Leitch.

In a few moments Ava returned carrying a tray on which platters were heaped with steaming food. It smelled good and it looked good.

'Hope you're hungry,' she said.

'If I wasn't already, I sure am now.'

She smiled and turned to go.

'Do you mind if I ask you something?' he said.

'No. Why should I?'

'It's about Cass Ryland.'

'OK. Go ahead.'

'That day his son died, you said it was unusual for

any of Ryland's men to come into town. As I recall, you said they were much more likely to spend time in Blue Bluff.'

'That's right. It's very rare to see anybody from the Hat R here in town. I've only seen Tim Ryland a few times.'

'How do you know they're more likely to show up in Blue Bluff?'

'I used to live there. I worked in the grocery store. Cass Ryland would collect his deliveries from there. I never liked him. He was rude and aggressive. People used to dread his boys showing up. Unfortunately that was quite often, because they used to arrive at weekends and blow off steam at the saloon.'

'Blow off steam?'

'That's putting it mildly. They were wild. They used to cause a heap of trouble.'

'What else do you know about Ryland? I mean, as far as Blue Bluff is concerned.'

'There's not much secret about that. It's pretty well known that he owns most of the town, including even the stage line. I think he must have had the marshal on his payroll, otherwise how did his men get away with behaving the way they did?'

'That's interestin'. Can you remember the marshal's name?' For a moment her brows puckered in thought but it didn't take long till she came up with a name.

'Langston,' she replied. 'Yes, that's it. Langston.

69

Like a weasel. At least, that's how I remember him.'
She gave the marshal a quizzical look.

'Just familiarizin' myself with the situation
regardin' the Hat R,' Dunbar said.

'Well, don't think about it too long,' she replied.
'Your dinner's startin' to get cold.' She walked away,
and he dug his fork into the mound of steaming
food.

The sun was climbing high. Cleadon, atop a slab of
rock, regarded the shimmering landscape through
his field-glasses. Suddenly he came to attention. In
the distance, still a long way off, he had picked out
something moving. He looked intently before
calling to Cayuse who lay full length on the ground
just below him.

'What is it?' Cayuse responded.

'I think we've got something. Come and take a
look.'

Cayuse struggled to his feet and climbed up
alongside his companion. He took the glasses and
stared hard in the direction Cleadon indicated.
After a few moments he saw dust and presently he
could discern a number of riders.

'You think it's them?' he asked, handing the
glasses back.

'Who else would it be?'

Cleadon took another look through the glasses.

'There's a bunch of 'em. Looks like Ryland's
taking no chances.'

'They got on to our trail pretty quick,' Cayuse remarked.

'If Ryland's so keen to nail us, it wouldn't surprise me if he's hired a tracker.'

He put the glasses down and they exchanged glances.

'Well,' Cayuse said, 'it seems like we were right. It ain't a matter of guesswork any more. Ryland is not far behind us and he ain't gonna go away. So what do we do now? Personally, I figure we've only got two options. Stay right here and take them on, or keep movin'.'

Cleadon looked about.

'It's not a bad spot, but I still wouldn't rate our chances very high. Even with the element of surprise.'

'I don't know. There's good cover.'

'Ryland isn't a fool. And if he's got a tracker on board, he'll likely work out places we might make a stand. But that's not what makes me think twice about tryin' it.'

'Oh no? What then?'

'We left Deerwood in order to avoid trouble. We've both seen enough of it. Speakin' personally, the last thing I want is more bloodshed.'

'So we carry on runnin'. Better make a start if that's the case.'

'I don't quite see it in those terms, but yes, for the moment we keep goin'. Maybe we can shake them off, or they'll lose interest.'

'You know that's not likely.'

'In the end it might come to a showdown. But the time's not yet.' Cleadon thought for a moment.

'Listen. Didn't you say there used to be a settlement somewhere up here in the hills?'

'Yeah. I guess it's just a ghost town now.'

'Then let's keep ridin' and see if we find it. With any luck, Ryland will pass it by.'

'Like I say, I think you're kiddin' yourself.'

'OK, I probably am. But let's give it a shot. If it doesn't work, and there's no other way out, we'll be in a better position to put up a fight than we can here.'

Cayuse didn't respond, and Cleadon took another look through the field-glasses. The band of riders was coming on inexorably. In the short time since he had last looked they had covered what seemed like a lot of ground. He could see now that there were nine of them. He was about to turn away when Cayuse seized his arm.

'Here, give me those glasses,' he said. He clapped them to his eyes and peered hard. Suddenly he chuckled.

'I might have guessed,' he said.

'Guessed what?' Cleadon asked in some surprise.

'That business of a tracker – well, I think you're right, and I think I know who it is.' He paused, and Cleadon said: 'Go on.'

'It's a fella goes by the name of Crow Jack. I've seen him around town from time to time. He used to do work for the Army. I can't be sure, but I'd be willin' to bet it's him.'

'Right. That's useful to know, but it doesn't make a whole lot of difference to the situation. If we're agreed, then I think we'd better start ridin'.'

Without more ado they slid down from the rocks and started gathering their things. It didn't take long till they had removed what traces of the camp remained and had saddled up.

'I don't figure we've done enough to fool somebody like Crow,' Cayuse said.

'Probably not, but we've done what we can.'

'Maybe we should just have carried on without stoppin',' Cayuse said.

'Who knows? I feel happier knowin' what we're up against.'

'I guess so,' Cayuse replied.

They climbed into leather quickly, touched their spurs to their horses' flanks, and hit the trail.

Marshal Dunbar had no clear idea of what he intended to do when he arrived in Blue Buff. It was only two days' ride from Deerwood, but he had only been there a couple of times before. Although of a similar size to Deerwood, it had the advantage of being on the stagecoach line. The service had been in operation a while. If Ryland owned it, as Ava had affirmed, he must have taken it over recently because Dunbar knew that at one time it had been run by a company formed by a group of the town's citizens. How had Ryland acquired it? Had he bought them out? It seemed odd, out of keeping with the note of civic pride the stagecoach had engendered. There had been talk not too long before of extending the line to Deerwood, but nothing had come of it. Had Ryland had something to do with the plan failing to materialize?

As Dunbar headed towards Blue Bluff, these thoughts were running through his mind. It was only after some time that he thought to ask himself why. Then he remembered what had happened recently, and Cass Ryland's part in it. He hadn't given a lot of thought to the Hat R previously. Events had brought Ryland to his attention, and he certainly didn't like what they seemed to reveal of the man and the way he operated.

A few scattered adobe shacks indicated that he was approaching the edge of town. The shacks gave way to more solid structures, and he was soon riding down the main drag with its rows of false-fronted stores interspersed with two-storey brick buildings. The town was like most others. The streets were quite busy, but it seemed to Dunbar that the atmosphere was subdued. People seemed either to avoid looking at him, or if they did so it was surreptitiously, and they quickly looked away again.

Although he wasn't sure exactly what he hoped to find, he had deliberately removed his badge of office, feeling it might get in the way. As it was, he was just another stranger in town. Maybe it was a false impression. He had spent a lot of time in the saddle and he was feeling tired and hungry. He decided to book into a hotel for the night and find somewhere to eat, once his horse was suitably tended to.

He soon located the livery stable. A wizened-looking oldster was forking hay out back. He looked up briefly as Dunbar emerged from the shadows, and then looked away again.

'Howdy,' Dunbar said. The man didn't reply. His jaw moved as he worked a chew of tobacco.

'Got room for one more horse?' Dunbar asked. It seemed a superfluous question, as there were only two horses in the corral. After a few more moments the man glanced at him again. If there had been a hint of irony in Dunbar's question, he didn't rise to it.

'You aim to be in town for long?' he said.

'Nope. Just passin' through.'

'Seems like a lot of people are doin' just that.'

'So what? You got some sort of problem with it?'

The man shrugged.

'Don't make no difference to me any more,' he said. For a moment he leaned on his fork and Dunbar was slightly taken aback when he suddenly laid the instrument against a rail of the corral and came closer.

'You got business in town?'

'If I have, it's none of yours.'

The man directed his gaze to Dunbar's .44s.

'You sure those guns ain't for hire?' he said.

'Like I said, I'm passin' through.'

It struck Dunbar that he wasn't making much progress with the ostler. At the same time, his vaguely aggressive manner suggested there might be a reason, which could be of interest.

'Look,' he said, 'I only intend stayin' in town for one night. I'm willin' to pay extra if you can guarantee you'll do a good job of lookin' after my horse.' The man seemed to relent a little.

'You don't need to do that,' he said. He pointed to a notice hanging on one of the walls.

'Those are the rates,' he said. 'All set out and legal. You don't need to make a special plea.'

Dunbar thought for a moment.

'If I get you right,' he said, 'you seem to be sayin' there's a lot of comin' and goin' in town, although it wouldn't seem to be the case judgin' by those empty stalls.'

'Ryland's boys don't need to put up here,' he replied.

Dunbar affected ignorance.

'Ryland? Who's Ryland?'

The oldster looked closely at him.

'No,' he said, 'you ain't havin' me on. I can see you're a genuine stranger in town.'

'You haven't answered my question.'

'Ryland? Cass Ryland owns this town. He's a big shot. Runs a big ranch goes by the name of the Hat

R. He uses this town as his playground. Leastways, his men do. Used to be a regular town once upon a time. Regular folks lived here, settled here. Not any more. A lot of them have gone. I'm one of the few old-time citizens still left.'

He paused.

'I shouldn't be tellin' you this. It probably ain't safe. But I'm too old to care now. I'm too old for Ryland to care about, either.' He spat a big globule of juice on the ground.

'Take it as a kind of warnin' if you like. Ryland ain't the kind to take to strangers.'

'And yet the town is on a stage route,' Dunbar replied. 'Doesn't that bring in some people from outside?'

'Used to,' the oldster replied. 'Not any more. Can't remember when the last stage ran. Almost seems like Ryland don't want any kinda truck with the world outside.'

'Why do you think that might be?'

'There are some theories.'

'Go on. You got me interested.'

The ostler glanced around him in a somewhat theatrical manner before shaking his head.

'No,' he said, 'I've said all I'm goin' to say. If you're so interested, try askin' around – if you can get somebody else to talk to you, that is.' He stopped to scratch his chin.

'I guess I musta took to you,' he said. 'But you ain't foolin' me. It's up to you if those guns are for

77

hire. I reckon you'll make some money. That's one thing Ryland ain't short of.'

Dunbar considered his words for a moment.

'You seriously think I'm hirin' myself out as a gunman? Hell, that's not the case at all.'

The oldster chuckled.

'We'll see,' he said. 'I'm an old man now. None of it concerns me any more.'

Dunbar looked at him again.

'You really mean that?' he asked.

By way of reply, the oldster picked up his fork once more.

'Go get your horse,' he said. 'He'll be fine with me.'

'One more thing,' Dunbar said.

'Oh yeah? What's that?'

'You couldn't recommend a place to stay?'

The man stopped to think for a moment.

'Did you say you were only stayin' for one night?'

'That's my intention,'

'Then you could do worse than try Adie's Lodgings on Chestnut Street. Turn right outa here and keep on goin' till you reach a cross-street. That's Chestnut.'

'I'm obliged.'

'Like I said, we don't get a lot of travellers. Generally, they just naturally head for the Regent Hotel, but they'll overcharge you. Like most everythin' else, it's owned by Cass Ryland.'

As he left the livery stables, Dunbar was feeling

fairly satisfied with what he had learned so far. Despite his initial hostility, the oldster had opened up, and he had been unable to conceal his dislike of Cass Ryland; even the mere mention of Ryland's name had betrayed this. A picture of that gent was emerging more and more clearly in Dunbar's mind, and it wasn't a pleasant one.

One thing in particular now gave him pause for thought. The ostler had assumed that his guns were for hire, and only one person would be likely to be doing the hiring: Cass Ryland. What sort of man would be in the market for hired guns? For a few moments he toyed with the idea of putting it around that he was available and seeing what would happen. Then he remembered who he was, and that Ryland would certainly recognize him. Once again he felt fearful for his friends Cleadon and Cayuse if that was the sort of man they were up against.

CHAPTER FOUR

Ahead of Cleadon and Cayuse the trail seemed to be coming to a dead end where a high wall of rock lay across the trail.

'I've got a feelin' we took a wrong turn some-where,' Cleadon said.

'I reckon you're right,' Cayuse replied.

'It wouldn't be hard to do. There were a few places where the trail seemed to peter out some.'

'There were cross-trails. They didn't seem to be leadin' anywhere, but who knows?'

Cleadon laughed.

'What are we talkin' about?' he said. 'It ain't as if it makes any difference to us one way or the other.'

Cayuse grinned.

'Yeah. I guess, for us, there is no wrong trail and no right.' He looked ahead.

'Still, I don't figure this looks too promisin'.'

They carried on riding. As they got closer, they saw that the wall of rock, which had seemed to present an impenetrable barrier, in fact had a narrow opening in its face. It was barely wide enough to allow the passage of their horses in single file, and took a sharp turn immediately they were through it.

'A keyhole pass,' Cayuse commented. 'It would have been easy to miss it.'

On the other side the cleft led to a narrow, winding defile. Cleadon looked up at the rock walls, which seemed to lean together to enclose them.

'Could make a good place for an ambush,' he remarked, 'if Ryland and his boys ever got this far.'

Cayuse raised his eyes.

'Too steep,' he said, 'and there's no cover.'

They moved slowly down the defile. It took another turn and then the rock walls began to fall away. The trail was descending quite sharply, and they were thinking of dismounting and leading the horses when the narrow passage opened up quite abruptly to disclose a shallow valley surrounded by low hills with higher peaks towering in the distance. A thin skein of river ran through it, with occasional streams running down the flanks of the hills and joining it at intervals. They sat their horses, taking in the view. Eventually Cleadon took the field-glasses and put them to his eyes. In the near distance, beside the river, he could see what looked like horse troughs, and when he raised his head, some wooden structures partly obscured by trees further off, beyond which were taller buildings. He passed the glasses to Cayuse.

'Tell me what you see?' he said. Cayuse took a close look before turning to Cleadon.

'Could be the ghost town,' he replied.

'That's what I was thinkin'.'

'Whatever it is, it's evidence that people have been here.'

Cleadon nodded.

'Well,' he said, 'now we've got this far, I guess there's no option but to ride on down and take a closer look.'

Cayuse handed the glasses back to Cleadon, who replaced them in their holder. They spurred their horses. Although they had been in the narrow canyon for only a short time, it felt good to be out in the open again. They both had the same sense of freedom. The path down was relatively easy. At the bottom they came through some trees and arrived at the river, where they dismounted long enough for the horses to drink. Then they rode on until they came to where a narrow tributary joined the river, and here they saw an object lying partly in the stream and partly on the bank. Cleadon realized it was what he had seen initially through the field-glasses, but its purpose was now apparent. It was the remains of a wooden trough. He drew up his horse and dismounted to take a closer look.

'Folks were obviously panning for gold along here,' he said. 'Look at this.'

He held up what looked like a box.

'The water ran into this. The prospectors shovelled dirt into the trough, and any gold would be caught against these cleats at the bottom.'

Cayuse nodded.

'Wonder if they found any?' he said.

'Sure they found some. Maybe a lot. Enough for them to establish a settlement of sorts.'

Cayuse looked up. The sun was shining on the river, which sparkled and glinted, but not like gold.

'You're right. Let's carry on and take a look at what's left of the place.'

Cleadon climbed back into leather and they continued on their way, following the banks of the stream. As they rode, they found further evidence of the prospectors who had once laboured there; the odd metal bowl, a broken rocker, the handle of a spade. In his mind's eye Cleadon tried to envisage what the place must have looked like back in those days, with men hard at work dipping their bowls into the sand and gravel of the river bed, or working in little groups, making use of a rocker to the same end. They were all gone now. If any gold remained, no one knew where. Suddenly Cayuse brought his horse to a halt.

'What is it?' Cleadon said.

'Over there,' Cayuse replied.

He was pointing to a log that lay athwart the stream. Partly concealed behind it was something that made Cleadon catch his breath.

'A skeleton,' Cayuse confirmed. 'Seems like not

all those old prospectors lived to tell their story.'

They dismounted and approached the remains. The bones were disjointed and had been partly gnawed by animals. Some scraps of clothing still remained. Cleadon hunkered down to take a closer look, but it was fairly obvious that the man had met a violent end. Part of his skull had been blown away.

'What do you make of it?' Cayuse asked. Cleadon stood upright again.

'Who knows? Maybe a fight over a claim.'

He got back on his horse, and after a moment they rode on again. The sight of the remains had unsettled them. The whole atmosphere of the place seemed to have changed. Although the sun still danced on the water, it felt oppressive and sinister. Neither of them spoke as their eyes sought for further signs of violence. And it didn't take long before they found the remains of two more men lying face downwards, and a further corpse on the opposite side of the river a little further down. From what they could make out, it seemed as if they had been killed while attempting to run. But what had they been running from?

'There's somethin' very much not right about this,' Cleadon said.

'Yeah. That first skeleton we saw might have been the result of a private feud, but this is somethin' much worse.'

They exchanged glances. Although neither of them gave voice to their concerns, they were both fearful of what they might find when they reached the settlement. After a few moments Cayuse broke the silence.

'What do you think?' he said. 'Some kinda dispute that got way out of hand?'

'Maybe. Or maybe. . . .' Cleadon paused.

'Maybe what?' Cayuse broke in.

'Let's not speculate. Let's wait till we get to the settlement. We might get a clearer idea then.'

Cayuse looked around.

'It's mighty lonely up here,' he said.

'Yeah. It's only by chance we stumbled on this way.'

'Looks like nobody's been here since . . . since whatever happened to those prospectors.'

Their horses' ears were pricked, as if they sensed that something was amiss. Unconsciously, Cayuse touched the scabbard containing his rifle. Shadows were beginning to stretch across the valley, and a breeze began to moan.

'Come on. Let's get to that ghost town before it starts gettin' dark.'

The terrain was becoming increasingly marshy, and they moved back through the trees. They had not gone much further when the course of the stream took a bend and they caught their first view of the settlement, a few outlying shacks. As they approached, their tumbledown and ramshackle condition became apparent. Lying in the grass they found a broken-down sign. The lettering was barely legible and it took them some moments to decipher it. It read *Lost Bucket*.

'A pretty appropriate name, I'd say,' Cleadon commented.

'If the place wasn't lost before, it certainly is now,' Cayuse replied. Beyond the shacks was an open patch of ground, and then more trees before they emerged on the banks of a narrow stream spanned by a broken trestle bridge. The boards were rotten and there was no chance of riding across it. Instead they splashed through the water, came up a gentle slope on the other side to find themselves at the beginning of what must have been the main street of the settlement. It was an eerie place, abandoned and silent apart from the soughing of the wind, the dull thud of their horses' hoofs and the occasional creak of leather.

They both felt nervous, and kept glancing from right to left as if the empty shells of buildings concealed some hidden menace. The outlying shacks and cabins had given way to more substantial buildings, but they were in a bad state, with their roofs fallen in and gaping holes instead of windows. Some had collapsed completely, and others seemed to hold together only by leaning one against the another like aged crones, or, stripped of their outer trappings, they revealed only their dark interiors.

'There ain't much left,' Cleadon commented, 'but it must have been quite a town in its heyday.'

As if to justify his words, they came alongside

what appeared to have been a hotel. Some faded lettering still remained, enough for them to decipher the name *Algonkwin*. They brought their horses to a halt and dismounted.

'Let's take a look,' Cleadon said.

They tied their horses to what was left of a hitching rail and climbed a rickety step. One of the batwings was missing and the other hung loose. They stepped through. There were a few overturned tables and broken chairs with missing legs. Debris littered the floor, in the middle of which a huge chandelier had shattered into a myriad of pieces. Behind what was left of the bar a mirror still retained a shard of cracked glass in one corner. It was the walls, however, which bore the clearest evidence of what had happened. They were riddled and pockmarked with bullet holes. At the side of the bar there were stairs, broken in places, leading to an upper floor. Stepping carefully forwards, Cleadon and Cayuse began to climb them. They led to a narrow passage with a torn and stained threadbare carpet, on either side of which were rooms with their doors open. With some trepidation, they entered the nearest one. A door at the end led to a balcony. Cleadon moved towards it.

'Be careful,' Cayuse warned. His voice was hushed and unnatural. 'The floor is probably rotten. You could plunge right through.'

With extreme caution, they both went through to the balcony. It was in a better condition than they had feared, but the surrounding rail was loose. Together, they stood looking out as the evening shadows began to descend over the desolate buildings and fill the dreary corners with a menacing shade.

'I don't like this place one bit,' Cayuse remarked.

'Me neither.'

'It's creepy. Even for a ghost town, it don't feel right.'

'Somethin' real bad happened here,' Cleadon remarked. Cayuse looked up at his companion.

'Hell, that's some understatement! I'd say those prospectors didn't just leave this place because the gold ran out,' he said.

'Yeah. They must have been driven out. The whole place has been turned over. We saw those bodies on the way in. I've no doubt that if we took a closer look, we'd find others.'

'I'm not sure I want to stick around long enough to do that.'

'If we're right, we owe it to those prospectors to try and find out more.'

'Find out more?' Cayuse repeated lamely.

'Find out who was responsible. They might have left some clues.' Cleadon looked out at the darkening scene. Below them, their two horses struck an incongruous note as the only sign of life in the grim desolation. When Cayuse spoke, he almost jumped.

'So what do we do now?'

Cleadon made a positive effort to get a grip of himself.

'Let's at least take a quick look about,' he said. 'Then, if you don't fancy stayin' any longer, we'll move on and find someplace to make camp.' He looked at Cayuse.

'I don't know about you, but I'm gettin' hungry. And I sure could use some good black coffee.' His words were meant to reassure his companion, but they lacked conviction.

'Come on,' he said, 'let's do it while there's still some daylight left.'

Carefully they made their way down the broken staircase, through the saloon and back outside. Cayuse made to move towards their horses, but Cleadon put a hand on his arm.

'Leave 'em where they are,' he said. 'We'll go on foot.'

The street was deep in dust. Their boots seemed to sink into it and kicked up little clouds in their wake. The battered old buildings seemed to watch them through their empty windows.

'I don't know,' Cayuse said. 'It's weird. We might be in Memphis as much as anywhere.'

'Memphis? Memphis, Tennessee?'

'No, I don't mean that. I mean Memphis, as in ancient Egypt.'

'Can't say I've heard of the place.'

'It don't matter. I just mean that bein' here is like bein' in a dead city, like it's somethin' from the past.'

'If what we found back there by the river is anythin' to go by, it is a city of the dead.'

They had gone only a little way when they came to a halt outside what seemed at some time to have been a bank. They exchanged glances.

'Might as well check it out,' Cleadon said.

They stepped through the open doorway. It was dark inside, and their eyes took some moments to adjust. When they did, they both visibly flinched. Sitting upright at the counter behind a broken mesh screen was the skeleton of a man held together by the worn clothes he still wore. He seemed to be staring straight at them and grinning with a sardonic smile. His arms rested on the counter and in front of him was a pile of coins which he seemed to be in the process of counting.

'Hell's a poppin'!' Cayuse exclaimed. 'What is that?'

Cleadon swallowed hard.

'I'm gettin' out of here,' Cayuse continued. He made to retreat, but Cleadon checked him.

'Hold it just a minute,' he murmured. He felt sufficiently calm to take a few steps closer.

'Looks to me like somebody's idea of a joke,' he said. He scrambled over the counter and bent over the sinister figure. There was a jagged hole in the man's jacket which told its own story.

'He's been shot in the back. Presumably some time later somebody set him up like this.'

Cayuse still held back.

'Why would anyone. . . ?'

He didn't finish the sentence. Cleadon took one more look at the grotesque figure.

'I figure I've seen enough,' he said. 'Let's go back to the horses and get out of here.' He was about to climb back over the counter when he was struck by another thought.

'Hold on a moment,' he said.

'What do you mean, *hold on*? I don't want to spend another second in this place.'

'Me neither. But there's a room back here and I figure I'll just take a look.' He didn't wait for a reply but ducked through the doorway. Inside, the room was even darker, but he could see enough to tell that it must have been the main office. An open safe lay on its side. Quickly crossing to it, he hauled it upright and bent down to peer within. He wasn't expecting to find anything, but to his surprise there were still a few bills and papers. Snatching up the papers, he went back out and climbed over the counter.

'Come on,' he said. 'I think we've seen enough.'

Outside, the last remnants of daylight were vainly holding the darkness at bay. Without thinking, Cleadon stuffed the papers into a pocket of his jacket as they made their way back to the horses, which were nervously lifting their heads and sniffing the air. They swiftly untied them and climbed into leather.

'Where to?' Cayuse asked.

91

'I don't care, just so long as we get out of this place,' Cleadon said. Without more ado, they turned and began to ride away, following the line of the street till it petered out into the surrounding wilderness.

Dawn was breaking when Cass Ryland awoke from a troubled sleep. For a few moments he struggled to realize where he was, but as full consciousness returned he became aware of another figure close by him. Instinctively he reached for his gun, but stopped when a voice spoke to him in sibilant whispered tones out of the darkness.

'It's OK, Cass. It's only me.'

'Leitch!' Ryland replied.

'Yeah.'

With a little effort Ryland sat upright and peered closely at the dim figure of his foreman.

'What are you doin'?' he said. 'You might have got your head blown off. Isn't it a mite early to be creepin' about?'

He looked away at the recumbent forms of his men gathered round the dead embers of the camp fire a short distance away, as if to reassure himself they were still with him.

'Sorry,' Leitch replied. 'I didn't mean to startle you. But there's something I figure you need to know before things get stirrin'.' He paused.

'Go on then,' Ryland urged. 'What is it?'

'Crow Jack has gone.'

There was no reply for a moment. Ryland's look of incomprehension was rapidly replaced by a lowering scowl.

'Gone?' he repeated. 'How do you mean "gone"?'

'Up and left.'

'How do you know he ain't around? Maybe he just woke early and went for a walk.'

'His horse ain't there. And he's taken some of our supplies.'

With an oath Ryland flung off his bed gear and got to his feet.

'That low-down dirty critter,' he said. 'I knew he was up to no good.'

'I don't see why he would do it. What does he get out of it? He ain't even been paid yet.'

'I don't care. I just want him found. I suspected he was leadin' us on a wild goose chase all along.'

Ryland made to go and wake up the men, but Leitch pulled him back.

'What the hell are you doin?' Ryland hissed.

'Wait a minute,' Leitch said. 'Think for a moment. Crow Jack had no reason to lead us on a wild goose chase. If we're here now, it's because Cleadon and Cayuse came this way. We must be close to them. It's my bet they're hidin' out in that ghost town.'

'In that case. . . .'

'Yes. In all likelihood they'll have found the remains of those prospectors we killed.'

93

Ryland's features collapsed in an ugly grin.

'Good luck to them,' he said. 'There's no way they'll find out who did it.'

'Maybe not, unless. . . .'

'Unless what?' Ryland interrupted.

'Unless someone tells them.'

'Someone tells them? Who's goin' to do that?'

'Crow Jack. He knows.'

'How could he know?'

'We haven't been entirely discreet. Our tongues have been a bit loose, especially since we got into these hills and it became apparent in what direction we were headin'. He probably overheard some of the things we've been sayin'.'

'We haven't said much. Not explicitly.'

'Maybe not you and me, but I wouldn't like to vouch for the rest of the boys. Who knows what they might have given away?'

Ryland paused to consider his words. A little below them, his men were beginning to stir.

'If you're right,' he concluded, 'then that's all the more reason why we've got to catch up with Crow Jack and eliminate him.'

'I agree. And the place he's most likely to be headin' is that ghost town. That's where he'll go to find the evidence.'

'He might have been scared off.'

'You're right. That's probably why he's done a runner. But he's a wily bird. If he can find evidence to back up his story, who knows what he might do?

He could blackmail us. A big payoff, or he tells the marshal.'

Again, Ryland took a few moments to consider.

'OK,' he said. 'I guess we might as well head that way as anywhere else.'

'And remember, if we're right about this, we should catch up with Cleadon and his *compadre* as well.'

Ryland chuckled.

'Three birds with one stone,' he said. He glanced at his foreman.

'Do you think you can find the way to the ghost town?' he asked. Leitch lifted his head as if to scent the air and looked all about him.

'I think I recognize the terrain,' he said. 'If we follow the river, I figure we can't go wrong.'

'Then I suggest we start movin' as soon as possible,' Ryland said. 'If Crow Jack left in the night, he can't be too far ahead of us. We might even pick up his sign.' Leitch nodded.

'I'll go roust up the boys,' he said.

He had no confidence that they would detect Crow Jack's trail, but he trusted in his judgement that the ghost town was where they would find both him and their original quarry. In a strange sort of way, he was relishing the whole situation.

Marshal Dunbar did as the ostler suggested and put up for the night at Adie's Lodgings on Chestnut Street. It proved to be good advice. In the morning, after a good breakfast, he made his way to the livery stable to express his thanks, but although the place was open, there was no sign of the ostler. His horse was standing in its stall and he checked that it was in good shape before making his way back into the street. He could think of nothing better to do for the moment than take a stroll around town. It was only as he approached the marshal's office that he suddenly remembered what Ava had said to him about the marshal being in the pay of Cass Ryland. That had been some considerable time before; maybe things had changed since then, and it was a different man in charge. What was his name? He thought back to the conversation he had had with Ava. Langston. That was the name she had given him. He had almost gone past the marshal's office when he stopped in his tracks and, after a moment's hesitation, put on his badge, mounted the boardwalk and knocked on the marshal's door. There was no reply, and he knocked again. In a moment the door was flung open and a figure wearing a silver badge appeared in the door frame.

Any doubts he might have had about the identity of the marshal were instantly put aside. How had she described him? A weasely sort of man? The person in front of him was small-legged, short and slim. He even carried a whiff of an unpleasant odour about him. The marshal looked him up and down before saying in a high-pitched tone:

'Who the hell are you? And what do want?'

'Marshal Langston?' Dunbar queried.

'What's it to you?'

'As you can see, I'm wearin' a marshal's badge just like you. Thought I might stop by while I was in town and pay a professional visit.'

'OK. You've paid your visit. It's been nice to meet you.' He turned and made to slam the door, but Dunbar inserted himself before he could do so.

'What do you think you're doin'?' Langston snapped.

'You're attitude ain't exactly friendly,' Dunbar replied. Langston turned his back, walked over to his desk and took up his seat behind it.

'I won't take up much more of your time,' Dunbar said.

'You're right. In fact, you won't take up any more of my time.' Dunbar took a glance around the room. Apart from the desk and a couple of chairs, it was bare apart from a cabinet in a corner, on top of which stood a half empty bottle of whiskey.

'I can see that you're busy,' Dunbar said.

'What are you doin' here?' Langston replied.

Taking advantage of the slight lapse in the other's stonewalling attitude, Dunbar advanced and straddled the remaining chair.

'We're meant to be on the same side,' he said.

'Just answer my question and then git.'

'OK. I'm here because I'm makin' some enquiries about a local landowner and rancher. I expect you probably know him.'

He paused to see if his words had produced any effect, but Langston's features registered nothing but the same cold hostility.

'His name is Ryland, Cass Ryland.'

Dunbar watched the other's face, but there was still no sign of a response.

'Are you pretendin' you don't know him?' he said. 'If so, you must be the only person who doesn't, since he owns most of this town.' A few more moments passed before Langston finally responded.

'I know Cass Ryland,' he replied.

'Good. Then maybe you can tell me somethin' about the way he operates.'

'I don't follow you,' Langston said.

'Well, for one thing, I hear some of his boys come into town on a regular basis and make a nuisance of themselves.'

'I've had no problems with any of Mr Ryland's employees.'

'Is that because you're one of them?'

'What do you mean by that?'

'How did you get to be the marshal? Did the townsfolk vote you in?' Dunbar raised his eyes to the half empty bottle of whiskey. 'Somehow, I doubt it.'

Suddenly, without warning, Langston pushed his chair aside and leaped to his feet. A gun appeared in his hand.

'I don't have to answer to you,' he said.

'Remember, I'm a United States marshal. Duly sworn in.'

'Get out,' Langston barked. 'Get out, before I put you under arrest.'

'On what charge?'

'Never mind any of that. Just get out. Now.'

Dunbar swung his leg over the chair and stood upright. Briefly, they faced each other before Dunbar made for the door.

'I'm leavin',' he said, 'but I might just stick around for a while. Who knows, maybe I can join in the fun when Ryland's boys hit town.'

'Keep out of my way. I'm warnin' you. . . .'

'About what? What are you goin' to do?'

'Just take my advice and don't let me see you again.'

Dunbar grinned. He opened the door and stepped out into the sunlight. The street was quiet. The same air of repression seemed to hang over it. A woman passed by holding a child by the hand, but neither of them looked at him. When he passed a young man further down the street, the man moved aside and seemed to give a sidelong look at his .44s. For a time he wandered aimlessly till he saw that his steps were taking him in the direction of a saloon, but when he got near he changed his mind about going inside. Instead, he began to make his way to the livery stable. He had had enough of the place.

When he got there the ostler was back. He felt an

odd sense of relief, as if he had been half expecting that something bad had caused his earlier absence.

'How was Adie's?' he asked.

'Good. Thanks for suggestin' it.'

'You're leavin' town already?'

'I think I've seen enough,' he replied.

The ostler stroked his chin.

'You went to see the marshal,' he said. It wasn't a question. Dunbar looked at him with some surprise.

'How did you know that?'

'Someone saw you. News travels fast.'

'There's not much newsworthy about that.'

'There is when someone goes there voluntarily.'

'The marshal isn't popular?'

'I ain't sayin' anythin' more.'

'Why not? Because you don't want to get into trouble?' The ostler shrugged.

'You don't need to say anythin' more,' Cleadon said. 'Just let me get my horse.'

The ostler led the way. Even judging by the man's back, Dunbar realized he wasn't going to get anything more out of him. He paid up and led his horse outside, where he climbed into the saddle.

'So long,' he said. 'It's been nice meetin' you.'

He rode off slowly, turning just once to see if the ostler was still there, but he had gone. He wasn't heading in any particular direction, but his route took him past the guest house where he had stayed the previous night. A man was standing in the doorway talking to someone inside whom he couldn't see. It didn't concern him and he barely registered it. Soon he was out of town, and after riding a short distance without an objective, he turned and set his course for Deerwood.

He rode slowly, partly for the sake of his horse, and partly because he was uncertain about what he should do next. He had gathered enough information about Cass Ryland for his doubts about him to be confirmed both by what the ostler had reluctantly told him, and by the attitude of the marshal. He was convinced that Ava was right and that he was in the pay of Ryland. In particular, the ostler's assumption that he was a hired gun tied in with his identification of Leitch from the old Wanted poster. He had a feeling that there was more to his suspicions, that there was a depth of infamy he hadn't yet plumbed. Where had Ryland acquired his wealth? Leitch was wanted for a number of bank hold-ups. Was that the source of Ryland's money?

The day was drawing down when he decided to set up camp. Although his lodgings the previous night had been more than satisfactory, thanks to the ostler's recommendations, he was nevertheless glad to be clear of Blue Bluff. The whole atmosphere of the town had been depressing, and a night under the stars had its appeal. Suddenly he found himself thinking of what he had seen as he rode past the guest house. There was nothing particularly remarkable about two people having a conversation on the doorstep, but for some reason it had assumed some significance. As he looked for a place to camp, his right hand unconsciously dropped down as if to loosen the thong that held his six-gun in place before he realized what he was doing. A grin lifted the corners of his mouth as he addressed the roan:

'Gettin' kinda jumpy. I figure you and I could use some rest.'

He set up camp beside a grove of trees where a stream trickled down a slight incline. As always, and without even thinking about it, he made sure he had a view over his back trail. He built a fire and threw some bacon into the pan. He made beans and coffee, and when he had finished eating he lay back with his head propped against his saddle and rolled a cigarette. In contrast to his previous mood, he felt contented and relaxed. An orange moon swam over the horizon, and as the blackness thickened, a swarm of stars filled the sky. His own camp fire was like a feeble attempt at a response, or an even more feeble challenge. Wasn't that what living was all about – a response, a challenge to an uncaring universe? But just now he didn't feel that way. After the stifling effect of the town, the open spaces seemed more friendly, even welcoming. He felt peaceful and he didn't know why, except that his belly was full and he was warm in the glow of the flames. He finished one cigarette and then lit another. As he did so his horse stamped and then whinnied.

'Quiet, boy,' he whispered.

He could see its dim outline against the outer darkness. It moved and seemed to be restless. Pouring the last dregs of the coffee on to the flames, he walked over to it. Its nostrils were flared and its ears were tipped forwards. He recognized the signs that it sensed an intruder, and in an instant his own attitude changed. He listened carefully, alert and attentive to any sound. He could hear nothing except the soughing of the wind and the dwindling crackle of the fire. His own senses now warned him of danger. Quickly he drew his six-gun, and instead of returning to the fire, slunk soundlessly into the surrounding undergrowth from where he had a clear view of the camp site.

He hadn't long to wait. After a few taut minutes a shadowy figure emerged, blending with other shadows that flickered in the dying firelight. Briefly he lost sight of it, and then his eyes caught a glimpse again as it moved, crouched low so that for a moment he thought it might be some wild creature that had gained entry to his camp. The figure moved slowly and stealthily towards the spot he had recently vacated where his bedding and his saddle could barely be discerned. Tense and coiled as a spring, Dunbar held back as the figure stood upright and a flicker of light was reflected from the barrel of the gun it held in its hand. The moment had come. Like a clap of thunder, Dunbar's voice rang through the night.

'Stop right there and drop the gun!'

The man wheeled. A stab of flame lit up the clearing, and with a crash a bullet went winging into the bushes, then another and another. The man's sense of direction was good and the slugs were uncomfortably close. Taking careful aim, Dunbar fired once and the man went spinning round. He fell to the ground before struggling to one knee and raising his gun once more. He was too late: Dunbar was upon him. Swinging his boot, he kicked the weapon from the man's hand and then stood over him with his .44 pointed directly at the man's chest.

'OK,' he snarled. 'You'd better start talkin'.'

'I'm hit,' the man moaned.

'Too bad,' Dunbar replied.

He looked more closely. There was blood flowing from the man's shoulder, but he didn't appear to be seriously wounded.

'I'm bleedin' bad. It hurts.'

'Not as much as it's gonna do unless you tell me just exactly what you're doin' here.'

The man writhed and his face was creased in pain.

'You've got it all wrong,' he muttered.

'Got what all wrong? I'd say there wasn't much room for doubt.'

'It's not the way it seems. I came here. . . .'

104

'You came here to kill me. That much is obvious. What I want to know is the reason why.'

'It's not true. . . .'

Dunbar bent down and seized him by his jacket. The man cried out in pain.

'Tell me one thing and I might go easy on you,' Dunbar said. 'Who sent you?'

He let go his hand and the man slumped back, whimpering. Dunbar had spoken with the intention of giving the man a glimmer of a chance that he might escape the worst consequences of his actions. In order to encourage him further, Dunbar asked:

'Was it the marshal?'

The man nodded.

'There's more to it, though, isn't there? Who are you? Who do you work for?'

'Please,' the man said, 'I need help.'

'Maybe you'll get it if you tell me the truth.'

The man seemed to be losing consciousness, and Dunbar bent over to slap him across the face.

'What? What is it?'

'I asked who you work for?'

'I don't . . . OK. I work for Cass Ryland.'

'So the marshal is in his pay too?'

'I don't understand.'

'Never mind. The marshal sent you after me. Why?'

'He said you were the man who killed Ryland's son, that you did it in cold blood.'

'You believe that?'

The man didn't reply. He was slipping into unconsciousness again.

'Wait a minute,' Dunbar said. He went quickly to his horse and pulled a flask from his saddlebags.

'Here, take a nip of this.' He held the flask to the man's lips, and he sipped the whiskey. It seemed to revive him a little. Dunbar repeated the question he had previously asked.

'The marshal works for Ryland too, doesn't he?'

'If you mean did Ryland support his runnin' for office. . .'

'He's Ryland's stooge, isn't he?' The man nodded his head again.

'How long have you worked for Ryland?' Dunbar asked.

'I don't know.'

'A long time?'

'I guess so.'

'Then maybe you know where Ryland got his money from?'

'I don't know anythin'.'

'I don't believe you.'

As if in exasperation, Dunbar made to lift the man from the ground, but it was unnecessary. Through his pain and waning consciousness he began to sob.

'I never wanted things to go so far. I wasn't responsible.'

'What things?'

'Those prospectors. I thought it was a matter of

taking some of their gold. I never imagined. . . .'

'Go on. What were you goin' to say?'

'In the hills. The prospectors.'

'You mean the Lost Bucket gold prospectors?'

'They didn't just give up and go away. Ryland drove them out. That's where he got most of his money from.'

Dunbar was inclined to ask further questions, but the man was clearly in a bad way and barely conscious. He took a moment to think. Although there were some unanswered questions, he had all the information he needed. His course of action was becoming clear. He needed to get up into the hills as quickly as possible and find out if what the man had told him was true. He had no doubt that it was, but it needed evidence. He looked at the sorry figure lying in front of him, and quickly came to a decision.

'Listen,' he said. 'You're right. You need a doctor. If you let me, I'll do what I can to staunch the blood and bind up that wound, and if you think you can ride, I'll take you back to Blue Bluff.'

The man groaned. 'I don't think I can do that,' he said.

'I think you can. Where's your horse?'

'Tethered further back. Along the stream.'

'I'll find him. Then I'll take a look at that shoulder.'

Dunbar walked off, taking care to pick up the man's gun on his way. It didn't take long for him to find the horse, and when he came back with it, the man had finally passed out. It made things only slightly easier.

CHAPTER FIVE

Daylight. Bacon sizzling in the pan and the aroma of coffee. Cleadon and Cayuse were already feeling a whole lot better than they had the night before, and after they had eaten and enjoyed a smoke, they were in good spirits again. The air blowing down from the higher peaks was fresh and invigorating, but in the valley it was mild and they both enjoyed the sensation of stretching out in the early sunlight. Eventually Cayuse rose to pour them both another cup of coffee.

'Sure is a nice day,' he said. 'Especially comin' after yesterday.'

'Yesterday's gone,' Cleadon replied. Cayuse wasn't sure he caught his drift, but replied anyway:

'Sure has.'

Cleadon raised himself on one elbow and looked at his companion.

'Now that things have moved on, as it were, what would you say about goin' back to that ghost town?'

'I don't want to see it again.'

'Me neither. But think for a moment. Whatever happened to those prospectors, maybe we owe it to them to try and find out who was responsible.'

'How are we goin' to do that?'

'I don't know. There must be some clues. We might find something'. Cayuse didn't look too happy.

'How do we know what to look for?'

'We don't. But it wouldn't hurt to take another glance.' Cayuse sighed.

'Just when I was beginnin' to enjoy myself.'

'I take it that's an agreement,' Cleadon replied.

'Let's just not rush into it,' Cayuse said.

They followed Cayuse's suggestion, and it was gone noon before they stepped into leather.

'We'll be out of there again before it starts to be dark,' Cleadon commented.

'You bet. No matter if you decide different, I'll be long gone.'

They lapsed into silence as they approached the deserted town. The change in their moods combined with the clear daylight made it seem smaller. They rode along the narrow main street, their horses' hoofs kicking up dust, past the bank with its grim secret, past the hotel and a single side street till they had almost reached the trestle bridge across the stream, when they stopped.

'There ain't so much to it,' Cleadon remarked.

'What next? Take another walk?' Cleadon didn't

reply. Instead he was looking away down the stream.

'What is it?' Cayuse asked.

'Look over there. In the mud of the riverbank. Looks to me like hoof prints.'

He got out the field-glasses and took a quick look before handing them to his companion.

'I think you're right,' Cayuse said after a few moments' scrutiny. 'But who in hell would have rode this way?'

'I don't know. Let's go and take a look.' They rode down into the water and then along the bank till they reached the spot. Cayuse got down and took a closer look.

'I reckon whoever it was rode in the river and then came up out of it at this spot. There's not much trace of any sign once the rider got out of the mud. What do you make of it?'

'The only people who could be anywhere near here are Ryland and his men.'

'There was only one horse.'

'Then I guess he must have sent someone ahead. Whoever it is, it can only mean that Ryland is very close.'

Cayuse got back on his horse and they rode back up the stream and into the town.

'Ryland might have set a trap,' Cayuse said. 'His men could be right here in town. Maybe they're watchin' us right now.'

'I don't think that's likely. Even if they tracked us this far, they were some way behind us. Besides, we only got here ourselves yesterday afternoon. No, I think if anyone's setting a trap, it's going to be us.'

Cayuse drew his horse to a halt and Cleadon followed suit.

'You mean you've decided to face up to Ryland and his boys?' Cleadon nodded.

'I hoped that by comin' this way we might have shaken them off. But it looks like it ain't goin' to happen. They're after our hides and nothin' is gonna stop them.'

Cayuse whistled softly.

'Hell,' he said, 'seems like you're gonna be usin' those .44s after all.'

'Yeah. I thought I'd hung 'em up once and for all, but it looks like I was wrong.'

He turned in the saddle to look more closely at Cayuse.

'You don't have to be involved. There's still time for you to get away.'

Cayuse grinned and shook his head.

'Man, I wouldn't turn down the chance to fight alongside a legend like Dane Cleadon. I've just been waitin' for the chance, for the time you would finally decide to take a stand.'

Cleadon chuckled grimly.

'Never mind all that,' he said. 'Let's start lookin' at this place in good earnest and choose just where we do it.'

'What about the hotel? We'd get a good view of Ryland and his men from one of those balconies.'

'Maybe. I'd like to take a look at that side street. We haven't taken a close look at it. Might be an idea to check it out.'

They rode back to the junction and turned down it. It was much like the main street except the buildings were smaller and seemed even more dilapidated. It didn't stretch far, and they had almost reached the end where it ran out into the surrounding terrain when Cayuse's keen eyes spotted something.

'Don't do nothin' to attract attention,' he muttered, 'but I thought I saw a curtain move. The building on the right.'

Without looking up, Cleadon raised his eyes. The curtain was nothing much more than a torn and tattered red rag.

'If someone's up there,' Cleadon murmured through the side of his mouth, 'he's got us in his sights.'

'What do we do?'

'Hang on tight and ride like hell. Now!'

At his hissed command they dug in their spurs and their horses burst forwards. As they urged them on, shots rang out in their wake and bullets went singing and screaming over their heads. They were galloping full tilt and didn't draw rein till they were out of range.

'Jumpin' Jehosaphat, who in tarnation was that?' Cayuse said

'The same person whose horse's hoofprints we

saw by the stream,' Cleadon replied.

'He sure didn't waste any time showin' himself.'

'I aim to return the compliment,' Cleadon replied.

'We'd better not take any risks this time. I guess we'll have to try and sneak up on him somehow.'

'No need to do that. He must have left his horse someplace. It certainly wasn't tied up anywhere in town. If we can find it, all we got to do is sit tight till he comes back for it.'

'What do you think he was doin' in town?'

'I don't know, but we'll find out soon enough. Come on, that horse has got to be somewhere this side of town, and not too far away, either.'

Cayuse raised himself in his stirrups and took a look around.

'There's a bunch of trees over yonder,' he said. 'I guess that's as good a place as any.'

They rode down to the copse. As they drew near, the attitude of their own horses told them that they were on the right track, and it didn't take them long to locate the tethered beast. It was a blue-eyed paint.

'Crow Jack,' Cayuse said. 'I'd have guessed it was his horse even if I hadn't seen it through the field-glasses.'

'That's interestin',' Cleadon said. 'I wonder just what he's doin' here.'

'Like you said, maybe he was sent on ahead to scout around.'

'I doubt it. I reckon there's more to it than that.'

'What then?'

'There's no need to speculate. All we got to do is make ourselves invisible and wait till Crow Jack turns up.'

'If he does. He might be wise to what we're doin' and give us the slip.'

'Whatever he does, he's gonna need his horse.' Cleadon had another thought.

'Let's take a look in his saddle-bags.'

They slid from leather and approached the pinto. It was nervous but when Cayuse stroked it and muttered a few words in its ear, it quickly settled down.

'You seem to have a way with the critters,' Cleadon remarked.

'They don't call me Cayuse for nothin'.'

The horse wasn't carrying a lot of baggage apart from provisions.

'Looks to me like Crow Jack was prepared for a ride.'

'Maybe he had some sort of fall-out with Ryland.'

'I'd say that seems quite likely, but what would he be doin' in that ghost town? I'd have thought it was one place he'd steer well clear of.'

Taking care to remove any traces of their presence, they rode off a little distance, tethered their horses, and then made their way back by foot. They concealed themselves as best they were able, and settled back to wait.

Time seemed to pass very slowly. They had antic-ipated that Crow Jack would return fairly soon, but they were disappointed.

'Maybe he's waitin' till nightfall,' Cayuse sug-gested.

'I hope not. I'm bored and my back is startin' to ache.'

'Could be somethin' to do with that injury you sustained.'

'Nope. Just old age. Still, I figure we won't have to wait too much longer.'

'How do you figure that?'

'He won't want to leave the pinto any longer than necessary.'

The minutes dragged by. Cleadon was beginning to lose concentration when he noticed that the pinto's ears were pricked.

'Get ready,' he breathed. 'I think Crow Jack is here.'

They listened closely for any sound and their eyes were strained for a glimpse of something moving among the trees and brush, but they could detect nothing. It came as something of a surprise when the bushes parted and the figure of Crow Jack emerged into the open, carrying a rifle. If they had been ignorant of his proximity, however, the same applied to Crow Jack, and when, at a given signal, Cleadon and Cayuse stepped forwards, he was taken unaware as much as they had been. Their six-guns were in their hands and Crow Jack's response was to immediately throw his rifle aside and put his hands in the air.

'Don't shoot!' he said

'Nobody's gonna shoot. Nobody's gonna get hurt. Just keep your arms where they are and don't move.'

While Cleadon continued to keep Crow Jack covered, Cayuse returned his weapon to his holster and expertly frisked him. Crow Jack had a Colt Army revolver stuck in his belt and a knife inside his jacket. Cayuse removed them and picked up the rifle he had tossed aside.

'OK,' Cleadon said, 'you can lower your arms.' Crow Jack did so, stretching his shoulders in relief.

'Guess I got kinda careless,' he said. 'Comes of bein' out of the game for a long time.'

'What game would that be?' Cleadon said. Crow Jack shrugged.

'You're an old-timer. You should know.' He turned to Cayuse.

'Howdy,' he said. 'I ain't so sure about this hombre, but I recognize you.'

'Yeah. I know you too.' There was a moment's silence while they regarded one another before Cleadon spoke again, addressing Crow Jack.

'Well, I guess that about takes care of the pleasantries. Now you'd better explain what you're doin' here, and why you tried to blow our heads off back there.' Crow Jack grinned.

'Sure, but before I do, I don't suppose you've got

a smoke?' Cleadon nodded. He got out his pack of Bull Durham and handed it to the other man, who rolled a cigarette before passing it back.

'Why don't you join me?' Crow Jack said.

'Sounds like a good idea. How about you, Cayuse?'

When they had lit up Cleadon motioned for them to be seated. They took a few drags.

'Ain't this real friendly,' Cayuse remarked.

'Friendly enough for you to put that six-gun away?' Crow Jack said. Cleadon took a moment to think before holstering his gun.

'Don't think of tryin' anything,' he remarked.

'Why would I do that? I know all about your reputation. I guess you're still pretty quick on the draw.'

'I thought you said you weren't sure who I was?'

'I know enough.'

'Where did you get the information? From Cass Ryland?' Crow Jack grinned again.

'I think it's time you started talkin',' Cleadon concluded. Crow Jack looked from Cleadon to Cayuse. There was little to encourage him in their stern expressions.

'Look,' Crow Jack began, 'I'm sorry I took those pot shots at you back there. If I'd realized who it was, I wouldn't have done it.'

'Who did you think we were?'

'I took you for some of Cass Ryland's men. You know he's on your trail? Yes, I guess you do.'

'He wouldn't be if you hadn't led him here.'

'I can't deny that.'

'Why are you workin' for Ryland?'

'Money. He's payin' well.'

'And that's it?'

'He told me you'd killed his son. Cut him down in cold blood.'

'Is that what you think? Is that what people think?'

'Nope, I guess not. Leastways, not when I heard Cayuse here was involved. I know him sufficiently to doubt he'd be involved in somethin' like that.'

'Let me put you straight right now,' Cayuse intervened. 'Cleadon was in no way responsible for Tim Ryland's death. That young punk had only himself to blame. He called Cleadon out. Cleadon wasn't even armed. When Cleadon tried to reason with him, he drew his gun. Cleadon was tryin' to disarm him when the gun went off. You can tell that to Cass Ryland, too.'

'Take it easy. I believe you. If I'd had any reason to doubt you before, what I learned while I was with Ryland has put me straight.'

Cleadon looked at him sharply.

'Go on,' he prompted, 'what did you learn from Ryland?'

'I overheard Ryland and his foreman talking.'

'You mean a man called Leitch?'

'Yeah, that's the one. Maybe you noticed one or two corpses on your way here? Well, Ryland was responsible.'

119

'Are you sure about this?'

'It wasn't only Ryland and Leitch who talked about it. I heard stories from some of his men, too. That was what persuaded me to get away from Ryland. That's why I was in that ghost town. I wanted to see for myself if what I'd heard was true.' He looked up at Cleadon.

'I sure didn't expect to find anyone else nosing around there too!'

'You'd tracked us most of the way. You can't have been too surprised.'

'I figured you'd give it a wide berth. I figured you'd be miles away by now. In fact, I can't quite understand why you decided to head for the hills in the first place.'

'Never mind that,' Cleadon replied. 'The fact of the matter is we were lookin' for clues as to who might have killed those prospectors. Now you've given us all the proof we need. There's only one question now.'

'Yeah? What would that be?'

'Would you be prepared to swear about what you've just told us in a court of law?'

Crow Jack looked puzzled for a moment, and then broke into a laugh.

'Court of law!' he said. 'Hell, Cass Ryland and his men are right behind you. They could be goin' through that town right now searchin' for you. It's only a slim chance you'll ever get down from these hills.'

His words were received in silence till Cayuse broke in:

'We know all that. That's why we're taking a stand. Do you care to join us?'

Crow Jack let out another ironic laugh.

'You must be crazy,' he said. 'Nope, I've already washed my hands of this whole affair. Man, you're on your own.'

Cayuse was about to say something in reply, but Cleadon forestalled him.

'That's fine,' he said. 'This isn't your affair. This is between me and Cayuse and Ryland. You've every right to go. But can I ask you just one thing?'

'Yeah? What's that?'

'If we ever get out of this and make it back to Deerwood, will you testify against Ryland in a court of law?'

Crow Jack's grin slowly faded.

'OK. Sure,' he replied. 'But if you ain't back in Deerwood pretty damn soon, I don't intend stickin' around.' He scratched his head.

'What am I sayin'?' he added. 'If you ever did get back, it would mean there'd be no reason to testify in court. It's gotta be either you or Ryland, and I hate to say it, but the odds are mighty long in his favour.'

They had finished their cigarettes. The sun was getting lower in the sky.

'Does that conclude the matter?' Crow Jack said.

'For now,' Cleadon replied.

121

'Let me repeat,' Crow Jack said. 'I'm sorry I fired those shots at you, but how do they say. . . .'

'All's well that ends well,' Cayuse interposed.

'Yes, that's it exactly. All's well that ends well. Am I free to go?'

'Yes, you can go,' Cleadon replied.

'Might I trouble you for my weapons?' Cleadon and Cayuse exchanged glances.

'Take the knife and the six-gun. We'll hang on to the rifle till we meet again in Deerwood.'

'Then I fear it's the last I shall see of it.'

They got to their feet. When he had strapped his gun back round his waist and hidden the knife in his jacket, Crow Jack mounted the pinto.

'Good luck,' he said. 'You're sure gonna need it.' He touched the pinto with his spurs and it ambled away. When he had vanished from view, Cayuse turned to Cleadon.

'There's one thing I don't quite get,' he said.

'Oh? And what might that be?'

'Just how you ever intend to get Ryland anywhere near a courtroom.'

'That's a good question,' Cleadon replied.

'You figure Crow Jack will hold to his word? About appearin' in court, I mean?'

'I have a feelin' he will,' Cleadon replied. He looked back in the direction of the town.

'Right now though,' he said, 'I reckon we've got other things to worry about.'

After all the time spent waiting for Crow Jack to

arrive, it was with some relief that they returned to where they had left their horses and climbed into leather. It was only a short ride back, and though they were fairly certain that Ryland and his men would be unlikely to have arrived, they approached the town with caution. They were about to go straight past the building where Crow Jack had been concealed when Cleadon brought them to a halt.

'What's up?' Cayuse said.

'I'm just curious as to what Crow Jack was doin' here.'

'Probably nothin' in particular. He just happened to be in this building when we came by. I guess it could just as easily have been another.'

'You're probably right. Still, it wouldn't hurt to take a glance.'

They dismounted and tied their horses to a dilapidated rail. Cleadon looked up at the building. Its faded lettering indicated it had once been a newspaper office. Inside, a rusting printing press confirmed the fact, and lying about in the dirt and dust were a few faded copies of the *Courant*.

'Kinda grandiose for a little place like this, don't you think?' Cayuse remarked.

'Those prospectors must have had some faith that they were startin' somethin'.'

'Pity it had to all come to this.'

Cleadon bent down and picked up one of the old newspapers lying on the floor. His eyes quickly scanned the headlines: *Stock Stolen from Within Town. Setback In The Hills. Old Timer Dies. An Enjoyable Occasion.*

'Nothin' very interestin' there,' he commented before throwing it down again.

Stairs led up to the next floor, from which Crow Jack had fired on them. They went up, being careful where they planted their feet. Facing the landing was a room with an open door. They went through and found themselves in a bare room with a view over the street. Crow Jack's footprints were clearly visible in the dust. A desk, a chair and a cabinet were the only items of furniture. Cleadon crossed to the cabinet and opened the doors. Inside were several stacks of old, yellowing newspapers.

'Wonder how often they brought it out?' he said. 'There seem to be quite a pile of 'em.'

Cayuse was struck by a sudden thought.

'We've been lookin' for clues,' he said. 'Maybe there's somethin' in there that would back up what Crow Jack told us about what happened.'

'I see what you mean.'

'Maybe that's what Crow Jack was doin' here.'

'Or maybe it was just chance. Probably this is simply the first place he started lookin'.'

'Either way, it might be worth takin' a riffle through those old papers.'

'Well, we haven't got time right now. They aren't takin' any hurt in here. Once we've dealt with

Ryland, we'll come back, gather 'em up and take them away with us.'

Cayuse chuckled grimly.

'Don't you mean "if" we deal with Ryland?' Cleadon didn't reply, and they were both silent for a moment before Cayuse asked:

'What do you think? Is this as good a place as any to make a stand?'

'I'd prefer that hotel.'

'Me too.'

'Let's get back there and make ourselves ready.'

Cleadon closed the cabinet and they made their way outside. The sun had sunk in the sky.

'You figure Ryland and his boys will arrive today?' Cayuse said.

'More likely tomorrow.'

'Then that means a night in this spooky place?'

Cleadon grinned.

'I think that's the least of our worries,' he replied.

After leaving his would-be assassin with the doc, Dunbar wasted no time in getting away from Blue Bluff. It was early dawn when he hit town and the doctor was less than pleased, but a wad of dollars soon appeased him. There was little chance of running into trouble, and Dunbar was careful to avoid any risk of being seen by the marshal, but he still felt relieved as the town fell rapidly behind him. When he was satisfied that he was clear, he slowed the roan down and continued at a steady pace in the general direction of the hills.

As he rode he began to wonder whether he should have asked his attacker some further questions, but the man had been in no condition to answer them rationally. He had enough to go on – more than enough. If what the man had told him was true, and he had no reason to doubt it, the information was shattering. Until recent events, although he had instinctively disliked Cass Ryland, he had never had any reason to suspect him of foul play. Now the evidence against him was overwhelming. Much of it, however, remained circumstantial. Maybe he would find conclusive evidence when he reached the hills and had found that abandoned settlement the prospectors had built, but there was no certainty that he would do so. It was a long time since the prospectors had left the area. Not many people knew for certain where the old ghost town was located. He would just have to rely on luck and his own instincts.

His thoughts turned once more to Cleadon and Cayuse. Where were they now? Still keeping ahead of Ryland and his men? Would they be added to Ryland's list of victims? And what about Ava? The last time he had seen her she had seemed to be in a positive frame of mind and making good progress after her trauma at Leitch's hands, but could he be sure that she wasn't just putting a brave face on things? How many other nameless victims were there? How many others crying out for justice? It was his responsibility to make sure that their pleas were not ignored.

CHAPTER SIX

It was still night when Cleadon awoke. For a few moments he didn't know where he was, and then memory returned, and with it all his faculties. He lay listening attentively. Cayuse's heavy breathing indicated that he was still asleep. In the darkness he got to his feet, and by the faint gleam of light coming through the empty window frame, made his way out of the room and down the staircase. He stumbled over a loose tread but recovered without making any noise. Picking up his saddle, he went outside and, taking great care, moved round the side of the hotel to where he and Cayuse had left their horses in an overgrown field at the back. He hoisted his saddle on to the back of the mare and tightened the girths before leading it a little way from the building, where he swung into the saddle. Making as little sound as possible, he rode away, along the empty street, across the stream, and into the darkness. The silence was oppressive, and partly to relieve the tension and partly to justify himself, he spoke quietly into the horse's ear.

'It's for the best. Cayuse doesn't deserve any of this. It was me who got us into this mess. It's gotta be me that gets us back out of it again.'

The sun rose on a dull and grey morning. Swathes of a fine mist hung in the valley, shrouding the hills and filtering the light as if through a fine mesh. He followed the stream but at some little distance in order to stay clear of the trees, and, although he wouldn't have admitted it to himself, the sight of those mangled corpses which had given him and Cayuse the first intimations of the catastrophe that had occurred. It was a lonesome ride but he didn't intend going far.

He had thought hard during the night and picked the spot where he intended to confront Ryland and his gang: the point where the narrow defile they had ridden through the hills opened out into the valley. He was counting that Ryland would come that way. There was a possibility he might have found some other route in, but since Ryland had been following his and Cayuse's trail all along, it seemed unlikely. Maybe there was no other way so accessible. If there was, perhaps some of those dead prospectors would have escaped to tell their tale.

The terrain was rougher and more broken as he approached the line of the hills. He rode slowly and carefully in order to spare the horse and also to give himself a chance to choose the exact location he wanted. He found what he was looking for in a dry wash with an ample covering of brush. Bringing the mare to a halt, he dismounted and set about making a small fire. When he had it going he made coffee, but ate nothing more than some hard biscuits. He wasn't hungry, but there was something else too, something that went back to his old gunfighting days: anything that might give him an edge was worth taking into account, and an empty stomach was one of them.

When he had finished a mug of coffee he got to his feet to check his surroundings, but there was nothing out of the ordinary to be seen. He hadn't expected there would be: it was still early, and there was plenty of time for Ryland and his men to put in an appearance. He went over to his horse, which was cropping the grass, and stroked its long face and muzzle.

'Hope Cayuse isn't too scared waking up by himself in that ghost town.' He had left Cayuse a note with the briefest of details about what he planned to do, but he felt a little uncomfortable about having left him behind. Should he have taken the oldster into his confidence? But he knew what would have happened: Cayuse would have done his best to stop him, and he wouldn't have been able to shake him off. This was the only way. It was his battle, himself against Ryland and his thugs.

When he had finished his second cup of coffee he emptied out the coffeepot, rubbed it down to take off the soot, and put it back with the rest of his gear. He scooped dirt over the fire. Once satisfied that the last embers were extinguished, he took his Henry rifle out of its scabbard and checked it over. It was the same weapon that he had carried through the War. Then he took each of his six-guns and worked the spring on the hammer backwards and forwards a few times. He spun the cylinder before checking the loads. They were Colt Army .44s with a cylinder conversion for the use of metal cartridges. Although older than the Frontier or Peacemaker models, they had served him well in the past and he felt comfortable with them. The only trouble was that he hadn't used them in a long while.

He flexed his fingers. They weren't as supple as they used to be, and he sometimes had pains in the joints. How steady was his aim after all these years? How clear was his eye? Maybe he wouldn't have to put them to the test. In spite of what had happened to him previously at Leitch's hands, and all the evidence to the contrary, he was still hoping that Ryland might be open to reason, and that bloodshed might be avoided. But he was realistic enough to know it was only a very slim hope.

He holstered his six-guns and laid the rifle alongside him. It was a strange situation he found himself in, one he couldn't have imagined only a few short days before. None of it was his choice. Until Tim Ryland had appeared in Ava's eating rooms, he had been just another private citizen living an ordinary commonplace life in an obscure town, with nothing to distinguish him except for the past he thought to have laid aside. Now, like some wearisome burden, he was obliged to pick it up again.

His thoughts were straying to memories of those times when his horse snorted and began sniffing the air. It seemed to have caught some scent, and Cleadon was immediately alert. He put his ear to the ground, and after a few moments thought he could detect a faint irregular drumming sound. He waited, and it grew a little in strength. It could only be Ryland and his men, approaching through the defile. In an instant he was on his feet and moving up the length of the wash till he had reached a spot where he had a clear view of the trail leading into the valley from the shelter of the brush. He set himself to wait.

The minutes ticked by. He felt some satisfaction that, now the time had come, he was feeling completely calm and relaxed. He gave no thought to the outcome. It had been that way before, when he had dealt with hardened criminals and outlaws riding the owlhoot trail, or when he had cleaned up some lawless cow-town. If the situation had been as simple as it had been then, he felt he might almost have enjoyed it, but it was bit more complicated. He wasn't sure he had come to the right decision about Cayuse. At the same time, he felt some sympathy for Cass Ryland. Although he had been in no way to blame, he still regretted what had happened. He didn't intend to needlessly throw his own life away, but it was enough for him to feel obliged to give Ryland a chance.

He watched and listened, waiting for the first signs of Ryland and his men. The sun had burned up most of the mist, and the day was now clear and bright. Birds sang in the trees. A little distance away he could hear the ripple of the stream. Leaves rustled. Then his ears picked up the sound of voices and hoof beats. He concentrated his gaze on the hillside and presently the first rider emerged. He quickened. It was Leitch.

A second rider followed. He had a description of Ryland, but it was hard to determine from it whether it was him. What convinced him that it was Ryland was his manner and the deference the others seemed to show him as they emerged into the open and gathered behind him. There were some desultory comments, but mostly they were silent. A last rider came through and took up his station. That made five in addition to Ryland and Leitch. The numbers didn't add up. When he and Cayuse had observed them, there had been nine of them. Allowing for Crow Jack's defection, one was missing. Cleadon watched for a few moments, but no one else appeared. He couldn't afford to wait any longer. Putting the matter from his mind, he stepped into the open.

'Howdy, Ryland,' he said. 'I've been expectin' you.'

The effect was dramatic. Confusion and consternation showed on the faces of Ryland's men, and a couple of the horses sidled away till their riders brought them back under control. A voice shouted and Leitch's hand reached for his gun. Cleadon raised his rifle but already Ryland had clutched his foreman's arm.

'Easy!' he snapped. 'Remember, if it's Cleadon, I want him alive.'

'It's Cleadon all right,' Leitch snarled.

'Leitch is right,' Cleadon called. 'I'm Dane Cleadon. Now that we've cleared that up, I reckon you'd best say just what you're doin' pursuin' me like this.'

'You know what we're doin'. We're comin' after the low-down side-windin' coward who killed my son.'

'I didn't kill your son. There was a struggle and he shot himself.'

'You're a liar as well.'

'I'm sorry it happened. But none of it was my doing. He came after me. I warned him once before, but he took no notice. He drew his gun on me. I had no gun. I was tryin' to disarm him.'

'Lies, all of it,' Ryland snarled.

'Why would I be doin' this if it wasn't true? It would have been easy to bushwhack you, but I ain't no killer.'

'You're one against eight. You wouldn't have got away with it.'

Cleadon was about to respond when Leitch cut in.

'Where's your *compadre?*'

'You worryin' he might have you in his sights right now? Don't. He's not involved in any of this.'

Ryland licked his lips.

'I didn't come here to argue with you, Cleadon,' he said.

'You didn't come to take me back to face the marshal, either.'

'You're plumb right there. I've had enough of this. I'm tellin' you straight, Cleadon. By the time I've finished with you, you're gonna wish you'd never crossed the Hat R.'

'The Hat R now, is it? I tell you something, Ryland. I know where you got the money to buy the Hat R. Yes, and all your other enterprises. Whatever happens here, sooner or later you're gonna be brought to justice.'

Ryland's jaw was working as he attempted to keep a check on his rage. It was clear to Cleadon that he was in something of a quandary. He couldn't work out what Cleadon intended to do. The numbers were on his side, but if Cleadon resisted he might be the first in line for a bullet. And he wanted Cleadon alive.

'This little talk isn't getting anywhere,' Cleadon said. 'Why don't you and your boys just ride out of here before anybody gets hurt?'

Ryland turned to his men ranged beside him.

'What do you think?' he said. 'Maybe we'd better do as he says.'

He made to turn his horse but Cleadon's eyes were sharp and he didn't miss Ryland's upturned glance. Besides, he had been caught once before. As a thrown lariat uncurled above his head, he moved sideways, brought up his rifle and fired at the hillside where a man's torso was visible above some rocks. There was a cry as the man fell and the lariat missed its mark.

Expecting an instant response from Ryland's men, Cleadon didn't hesitate but threw himself into the surrounding brush and, taking advantage of their confusion, moved quickly back into cover. Whatever Ryland's orders had been, they were disregarded. As he slunk and slithered away, a crescendo of gunfire shattered the silence and bullets rained down on the place where he had been standing. They whined and screamed around him, but he had chosen his spot well and they were high and wide of their mark.

He could hear Ryland's voice above the cacophony of noise trying to order his men to stop firing. The shooting went on for a few moments and then came to a halt. He was thanking his lucky stars that for the moment he had escaped, but he knew Ryland's men would start combing the brush for him. He hadn't anticipated the man on the hillside, but now the numbers added up. Ryland was more astute that he had reckoned. Or was it just that one man had been further back than the others and taken up that position in the light of the situation that presented itself? Either way, he had his answer. There was to be no reasoning with Ryland. He had made an effort to bring about a peaceful solution to the matter, but it was in vain. He had no choice now but to battle it out. It was either Ryland or himself, and the odds were all in Ryland's favour.

Voices were calling to each other as Ryland's men left their horses and entered the brush. He crept forwards, drawing them away from the direction of his original camp-site where his horse was tethered. Gradually he changed direction and began to circle back on them. It was hard to determine just where they were. He was judging by the sound of their voices, but he had a reminder of how close one of them was when a shot rang out. He felt a shiver run up his arm and his rifle was torn from his grasp. With hardly time for thought he drew his six-gun. He ducked and then spun quickly to see a figure partly concealed behind a tree. Taking only a moment to steady himself, he opened fire and heard a groan as the man disappeared from sight.

His arm felt numb and he thought he had been hit, but then he realized that the bullet must have struck the stock of his rifle. He shook his arm a few times to restore its feeling. He'd had a lucky escape, but when he checked his rifle, it was too badly damaged to be of further use. He would have to rely on his .44s. It was doubly unfortunate because, in addition to losing his rifle, Ryland's men now had a much better idea of his whereabouts. He took a moment to reconsider the situation. His pursuers had ceased calling to each other. They probably realized they had a better chance of catching him if they stayed silent.

He had a sudden thought. Was it likely that Ryland would have plunged into the brush in search of him, or would he have left that to his men and remained where he was? The same question might apply to Leitch as well. If so, Ryland certainly wouldn't expect him to return to the spot where he had accosted them. He would expect him to try and make his escape. If he could wend his way back without being detected, he might be able to capture Ryland. Without him, the rest might lose interest and capitulate. Ryland was driven by an insatiable thirst for revenge. What motive did *they* have for continuing the fight? With nothing but a vague plan in mind, he began to make his way back towards the head of the wash.

There was plenty of cover, but he needed to take care. At one point he thought he detected movement and flung himself to the ground. He lay immobile till he was satisfied that if there had been anybody nearby, they had not seen him. He got back on his feet and carried on moving stealthily, feeling more confident that for the time being he had given his pursuers the slip. They would soon realize their mistake, but with any luck at all he might have a margin of time in which to change the situation.

He had to be more careful than ever because the concealing brush was getting thinner. He reckoned he was about where he needed to be, when he caught a glimpse of horses. They must be those belonging to Ryland's men. Was Ryland's horse among them? If it was, would Ryland be close by? He was unlikely to be alone. Someone else would probably be with him and keeping one eye open for Ryland and the other eye for the horses. He had a feeling of *déjà vu*. The situation was like the one just a short time earlier when he had first stepped out of his cover to accost Ryland and his men. Now he had a clearer view of the horses, but as yet he could see no sign of anyone with them. His brain was working fast.

He had another idea. If he could get close enough without being detected, he could spook the horses. Without them, Ryland and his men would be at a real disadvantage. More stealthily than ever, taking care with every step not to make a sound, he crept closer to the horses. Despite his best efforts, it was clear by their restless behaviour that they sensed his presence. Had anyone been left in charge? It seemed unlikely. Things had happened quickly. Ryland's men had dismounted in a hurry in order to pursue him. Taking a chance, he sprinted forwards, bent double to make himself as small a target as he could if anyone was around. It was as well that he did, because a stab of flame was immediately followed by the boom of a rifle shot.

The horses reared in panic and began to scatter in all directions. As one of them came by, he seized the pommel and as it picked up speed, got his foot in a stirrup and heaved himself on board. In the same instant he saw a man emerge directly in front of him but before he could do anything he went down under the horse's hoofs. The horse swerved and reared, and it took all of Cleadon's skill to bring it back under control.

Once he had done so he turned its head in the direction of where he had left his own horse, not wasting any energy looking back to see if the man had recovered. It wasn't too far, but he lay as flat as he could over the horse's back, expecting to be intercepted at some point, or be a target for fire from the surrounding brush. Several shots rang out and he could hear shouts above the pounding of the horse's hoofs, but he reached the place where he had left the mare, and quickly swapped over.

Without a clear idea of what he should do next, he began to ride hard, away from the immediate scene of action, back in the direction of the ghost town. He had set out that morning with the hope of being able to persuade Ryland to see sense. He hadn't worked out what his course of action would be if that didn't happen. Now he had even less of a plan, but he needed to come up with something quickly. Ryland must already have realized what had happened, and it wouldn't take long for him to gather his men, round up the horses, and be back on his trail.

His mare was beginning to blow so he brought it to a halt. He was half way back to the town and there was no point in going any further. He could think of no better option than to repeat his previous action. Riding into the trees near the stream, he got down, led the horse to the water and let it drink. Then he knee-haltered it and moved back among the trees. It couldn't be long before Ryland appeared. Losing his rifle put him at a disadvantage. If he had been cleverer, he could have picked up a rifle belonging to one of Ryland's men. He checked his six-guns and set himself to wait.

After a while his back began to ache. He realized that he had probably still not fully recovered from being dragged behind Leitch's horse. Apart from that, he was feeling all the wear and tear of the last few days. He was getting way too old for this sort of thing. He should be taking his ease at his own cabin back in Deerwood. Somehow that seemed a long time ago, almost as though it was in a different life. Or maybe he had never left his old life behind, maybe it was his life in Deerwood that was unreal.

His thoughts began to become blurred, and he realized he was beginning to nod off. How long had he been waiting? He glanced up at the sky. The sun was a lot lower than it had been when he last looked. Where was Ryland? He began to feel uneasy. Could he have missed him? It was unlikely. The trail he had ridden seemed the obvious one to ride, but there could be alternative routes, taking Ryland in the direction of the old ghost town. Was Ryland playing some sort of game? Did he guess that Cleadon would probably be waiting for him somewhere along the trail? He thought of Cayuse. Maybe it hadn't been such a good idea to leave him behind. Perhaps Cayuse was in danger now from Ryland.

Weighing things up, Cleadon came to a decision. There was no point waiting for Ryland and his men any longer. He couldn't be sure that they would come the same way. They might have already gone past him. He had to get back to Lost Bucket. If Cayuse was at any kind of risk, he needed to be by his side. If Ryland was aiming for the town, that was where the struggle would continue. If he wasn't, nothing would be lost. Without more ado, he returned to his horse, climbed into the saddle, and continued on his way towards the ghost town.

He didn't want to tire the mare unduly, but still rode at a decent pace. Worrying all the while that Ryland might have outmanoeuvred him, it was with a sense of relief that he approached the outlying cabins, rode down into the stream by the bridge and came up again on the other side. All the way he had been looking out for signs of Ryland's presence, but had not seen anything. Now as he rode slowly down the main street his eyes flickered from one empty building to the next, searching for danger. The dusty street bore the imprint of horses' hoofs, but as far as he could see they were caused by Cayuse and himself, and possibly Crow Jack.

For a few moments he reflected that Ryland might have gone away, that his men might not have relished the prospect of meeting with him now their numbers were reduced. The odds were still heavily in their favour. But no, he knew better than that. Ryland wouldn't rest till he had carried out his revenge.

Cleadon was hoping to see Cayuse's horse still tethered outside the hotel, but it wasn't there. He wasn't surprised. His guess was that Cayuse was out riding somewhere, trying to find him. He dismounted and took his horse round to the trees behind the broken corral where no one would detect it. Then he made his way back to the hotel, entered through the broken batwings and went up the stairs. This time he didn't stop at the first landing but went up a further flight of stairs to a loft with a trapdoor at the end. It was gloomy and dark, and he stumbled over various objects lying on the floor without bothering to look more closely.

A ladder lay underneath the trapdoor. He propped it up and climbed the few steps. Reaching up, he pushed at the trapdoor. It was stiff at first and it took a lot of effort, but he finally succeeded in forcing it open. With his arms and shoulders, he heaved himself through, on to the flat roof of the

143

building. He looked around. The place looked rickety. Maybe it wasn't strong enough to support his weight and he would fall right through. He crawled forwards on his knees, and then gingerly stood upright. He took a few steps. It was all right. The roof was sound. Now he had a good vantage point.

He made his way to the edge of the parapet, from which he had a clear view of the surrounding country. His eyes swept the wide panorama, but he could see nothing untoward. He sat down and once again checked his weapons. He took a further look. There was still no sign of Ryland, but after a few minutes his ears seemed to catch the distant clatter of horses. The sound died away, but he was certain that it was Ryland. He had brought his canteen of water from his saddlebags and took a swig. He glanced down. An afternoon wind had developed, blowing clumps of tumbleweed along the empty street. A few window frames rattled. He took another drink from the canteen. Something soporific in the atmosphere made him feel heavy and lethargic.

Then all at once he snapped to attention. The wind had shifted and brought the sound of horses' hoofs more clearly to his ears. He strained his eyes in the direction of the sound and saw movement. Some riders came into view through the trees on the opposite side of the town from which he had entered. There were three of them. Where were the others? He soon had his answer when he saw three more riders bearing down on the town along the river coming from the other direction. That made six of them. According to his calculations, there should at most be only five. Who was the extra rider? He took a closer look. It was Cayuse! They must have caught up with him somewhere outside town, and now he was their prisoner. It was down to him to do something about it.

As they approached the town, both groups of riders slowed almost to a halt. They were obviously very wary. They had no reason to suppose that Cleadon was anywhere close, but nonetheless they were nervous. The second group of riders, which included Cayuse, began to come on again, riding up the riverbank to the edge of town. They paused once more. Cleadon glanced the other way. The first group of riders were gathered at the opposite end of the main drag. Among them he recognized Ryland and his foreman, Leitch. Both groups began to move forwards. They would presently meet in the middle of town not far away from the hotel. Cleadon was thinking rapidly, trying to think of a course of action that would minimize the danger to Cayuse, but before he could work anything else matters were taken out of his hand when Cayuse's horse suddenly reared and then bolted forwards.

Instantly shots began to ring out in his rear. Realizing that Cayuse had made a break for freedom, Cleadon raised his six-gun and opened fire. The riders were still too far away for any accuracy, but he aimed to distract Ryland's men. It worked. Instead of aiming their shots at the retreating Cayuse, they looked up and opened fire on the rooftop. Cleadon cursed his luck in not having a rifle. Cayuse was hanging on grimly but to Cleadon's dismay the horse he was riding suddenly fell, hurling Cayuse from the saddle. Cleadon leaped to his feet, ran to the end of the rooftop and jumped over the parapet to land on the roof of the building next to it. It was at a lower level and took him closer to where Cayuse lay in the street. He continued firing as bullets screamed through the air and passed menacingly overhead. Coming to the opposite end of the roof he lowered himself over the edge to drop the rest of the way into the narrow gap between two buildings. Hurling himself forward, he burst into the main street close to Cayuse.

His horse had been shot, and the oldster had taken what shelter he could behind it. Cleadon's gun was empty. Holding his second gun, he knelt down and began fanning the hammer. The two riders held their ground for a few moments and then they reeled and rode away. Cleadon turned in the opposite direction, looking for Ryland and his two fellows, but they weren't there. For the moment, they must have taken shelter down the side street. Now he had the chance to turn his attention to Cayuse, who lay inert. He had lost con-

146

sciousness and it wasn't clear whether he was badly hurt or not. The immediate need was to get him off the street and into the shelter of one of the buildings.

Cleadon sheathed his gun, stooped low and lifted the oldster. As he did so the injured horse struggled to its feet and stood with its head hanging for a few moments before beginning to amble away. Cleadon struggled with his burden into the nearest building and, laying Cayuse on the floor, began to examine him when the oldster's eyes opened and he blinked a few times before fixing his gaze on Cleadon.

'Where in tarnation did you get to?' he asked. Cleadon grinned.

'Never mind that,' he said. 'Right now we've got other things to worry about.'

'I feel like I've been trampled by a wild mustang.'

'You're not far wrong.'

Cayuse struggled to sit up, groaned and sank back again, and then managed to do so with a bit of support from Cleadon.

'Give me a minute or two to get my breath,' he said.

'Those varmints were firin' at you. I was worried you might have been hit, but as far as I can tell you're still in one piece.'

'It doesn't feel like it,' Cayuse said. He looked around as if seeing his surroundings for the first time.

'I was out lookin' for you when I ran into Ryland. Kinda took me by surprise.' He gave Cleadon a quizzical glance.

'There were five of them. That's four less than I remember.'

'Crow Jack left them.'

'That doesn't account for the others.'

'Let's just say I ran into them myself,' Cleadon replied. Cayuse broke into a laugh, which sounded like more of a cackle. He sat upright and took a few deep breaths.

'OK,' he said. 'I guess we can leave the explanations till later. Give me a gun.'

Cleadon helped Cayuse to his feet. The oldster took a few unsteady steps before walking around the room a few times.

'Are you sure you're all right?' Cleadon said,

'I'm fine now.'

Cleadon drew his empty pistol from its holster and passed it to Cayuse along with his cartridge belt. They jammed bullets into the chambers of their guns.

'What now?' Cayuse asked. 'Do we go after them, or wait right here?' As if in answer to his question, there came a sudden burst of rifle fire and slugs slammed into the wall.

'Better take cover!' Cleadon said.

They positioned themselves next to the two window frames which gave them a view of the street. After the initial outbreak, the gunfire was sporadic.

Taking advantage of the lull, Cayuse raised his head above the level of the window ledge to take a look outside, but ducked immediately as a couple of shots rang out in response.

'They must have seen us enter the building. They've got us pinned down,' Cleadon said. Any further words were drowned as a fresh crescendo of noise brought a haze of bullets thudding into the walls of the building. Cleadon and Cayuse responded by getting off a few shots themselves, but they had no opportunity to take aim and were firing blind. Cleadon gave a signal to stop.

'Save the ammunition!' he called. 'We can't afford to waste any.' He was thinking rapidly. The situation wasn't good. He and Cayuse had a very limited supply of bullets for their six-guns. Ryland and his men had rifles and as much ammunition as they needed. Something had to be done.

'I need to know just where those varmints are,' Cleadon said. Cayuse nodded. Cleadon got down on the floor and slithered to the doorway. When Ryland's men began shooting, he peered outside. It took a few moments before bullets began to tear up the dust in front of him, but he had seen enough of the flashes of flame to pinpoint the building almost opposite where Ryland's men were located. He rolled away from the doorway and took up his station again.

'How many of 'em?' Cayuse asked.

'I figure at least three. Two downstairs and one

behind a window on the floor above.'

'Just the one building?'

'I think so, but I couldn't be sure.' A fresh burst of gunfire shook the building. When it had subsided Cayuse resumed:

'I got a feelin' you've been in situations like this before.'

'Sure, but I was a lot younger then.'

'Have you got a plan?'

Cleadon drew his head back as bullets tore into the wall all around the window frame. A single bullet went singing through the empty space and ricocheted across the room, sending up slivers of plaster.

'I need to get closer,' he said.

'Get closer! Are you crazy? You set one foot out there and you're a dead man.'

'We'll both be dead men pretty damn soon if we don't do something.'

'So what are you gonna do?'

'I need you to cover me while I make a sprint for that building.'

Cayuse shook his head.

'You'd be committin' suicide,' he replied. 'There's gotta be somethin' better than that.'

'Tell me what it is, and we'll give it a try.'

Cayuse thought for a moment.

'I don't know,' he said. 'But I can't go along with what you say.'

'Keep shootin'. There's an old horse trough

across the street. If I can at least make it to there, I'll have a chance.'

Cayuse let out a long sigh.

'This is not like your town-tamin' days,' he said. 'Those times are gone. For both of us.'

'Just keep me covered,' Cleadon replied. Without waiting any further, he moved to the doorway as another wave of gunfire shattered the air. Gun in hand, he waited for it to die down. When there appeared to be a pause, he looked at Cayuse.

'Are you ready, partner?' he asked.

'I'm ready.'

Cleadon nodded, and then, with his gun blazing, he hurled himself through the doorframe.

For a moment there was no response from Ryland's men and Cleadon was almost half-way across the street before they opened up. Bullets began to sing all round him, whining through the air and tearing up dust. He had taken them by surprise and their aim was erratic. Time seemed to stop – he couldn't tell whether it was seconds or hours till he reached the opposite side of the street, but he didn't stop for the horse trough or anything else. The door of the building where Ryland's men were concealed hung on its hinges and he crashed through, barely noticing the impact.

The two men inside who had been shooting wildly turned to face him. He saw fire like a red rose and something bit into his thigh, but he was a berserker and they loomed so large that he couldn't miss with his flaming .44s. They went down like corn before a hailstorm, and still he didn't stop. Up the stairs he charged, not noticing the broken treads.

He saw an open door. A man appeared. He saw the startled look on his face as he bowled straight into him, knocking his gun from his hand. His momentum was arrested and he stumbled as the man came at him, but his attacker was off balance and he easily avoided his swinging arm. Cleadon's own gun was empty. He threw it down as he ducked, and then came up suddenly, slamming his head under the man's jaw. There was a sickening crunch as the man staggered backwards. Cleadon gave him no chance to recover. In a moment he had sunk his right fist into his midriff and brought his left fist crashing into his cheek. The man went down and Cleadon stood over him menacingly.

'Where's Ryland?' he gasped.

The man looked up. His face was a bloody broken mess and he was gasping for breath.

'Where's Ryland?' Cleadon repeated.

The man shook his head. Cleadon himself was struggling to breathe. He suddenly felt drained and his head was dizzy. He leaned against a wall to steady himself. The man lying on the floor was whimpering, and the sound seem to grow louder until he realized it was something else: the sound of footsteps on the stairs. He pushed himself away from the wall and turned towards the doorway, trying to gather himself, when a voice rang out:

'It's no use, Cleadon. We've got Cayuse. One false move and he dies. Throw out your gun.'

He took a glance through the doorframe. At the head of the stairs stood Cayuse with Ryland and Leitch close behind him. Ryland held a gun against the oldster's back. Cleadon was fully alert now. Two guns were lying on the floor, his own and the man's. Quickly, he picked them both up.

'I said throw out your gun,' Ryland's voice repeated.

Cleadon moved to the doorway and threw out his empty six-shooter.

'OK. Now you.'

Cleadon slipped the man's gun into his belt and stepped outside. His eyes met Cayuse's. The oldster winked.

'You're bleedin',' Cayuse said. 'Have you been hit?' Cleadon glanced down at his leg, which was soaked in blood. Only then did he become aware of a throbbing pain in his thigh.

'Guess I must have been,' he muttered.

'Shut up!' Ryland barked.

In the same moment Cayuse threw himself forwards and Cleadon's gun jumped in his hand as he squeezed the trigger. Ryland gave a scream of pain, clutching at his shoulder as a bullet tore into it, and the gun fell from his hand. Cleadon turned to face Leitch, expecting him to open fire. Instead, to his surprise, Leitch turned and began to rush down the stairs.

'Keep Ryland covered!' Cleadon shouted.

As Cayuse seized Ryland's gun, Cleadon leaped forward in pursuit of Leitch. Ignoring his wound and the dangers of the rickety treads, he took the stairs two at a time, but Leitch had already reached the bottom and vanished from sight through the open door. Cleadon rushed into the street to be greeted by a couple of shots from Leitch's six-gun. When Leitch saw that he had missed, he turned as if to run on again, but stopped when he saw Cleadon's gun in his hand.

'I could drop you right now,' Cleadon shouted, 'but I'm gonna give you a chance. That's more than you gave me.'

'I don't know what you're talkin' about.'

'I'm talkin' about a little matter of an attempted lynchin'.'

'Look, I only do what Mr Ryland tells me. I ain't responsible for any of this.'

'I take it you're not responsible either for what happened right here in this town.'

'I ain't never been here before.'

'I'm sick of your lyin'. Like I say, I'm gonna give you one chance. I'll put my gun back in its holster. You do the same. Then it's all even, just you against me. I'm an old man now. You've got a good chance of beating me to the draw.'

'What if I don't do as you say?'

'Try raisin' that gun. You'll see what happens.'

Leitch licked his lips, undecided what to do. He was weighing his chances of being able to fire off another shot before Cleadon, but Cleadon's gun was already pointing at him.

'Look,' he said, 'why don't we talk about this?'

'The time for talkin' is over.'

Leitch still hesitated. He looked closely at Cleadon. It was true: he was an old man. His reflexes couldn't be so good. Reluctantly, he placed his gun in its holster and Cleadon did the same.

'Ready when you are,' Cleadon said.

They were long, long years since his town-taming days. He had been fast once. Time was when he would have backed himself against anybody. He had observed that Leitch was carrying his revolver in a low-slung buscadero-type rig. It was an indication that he wasn't entirely unused to slinging lead. However, one thing he had in his favour that counted as much as speed of movement: calm of mind was the equal of a fast draw, and he felt calm.

Leitch's right hand was hovering close to the butt of his gun and he watched it intently, waiting for the slightest movement. Some men looked for any sudden change in an opponent's expression but Cleadon had never operated that way. Leitch's hand loomed large in his sights; everything else was blotted out. He didn't see the twitch in Leitch's cheek or the drops of sweat on his brow. All he saw was that gun hand as it suddenly dropped. In an instant Leitch had drawn and his gun was spitting lead, but quick as he had been Cleadon was quicker. The bullets from Leitch's gun whined close but harmlessly over his head as Leitch staggered back, blood pouring from his chest.

As the smoke cleared, Cleadon steadied himself to fire again, but there was no need. This time he did look into Leitch's face, and what he saw was the emptiness in his eyes. They were already blank and he knew that Leitch was not seeing anything any more. For a moment Leitch seemed to recover his equilibrium but then he fell forwards, hitting the ground with a thump where he lay lifeless, his blood staining the dust. As if in a dream, Cleadon put his six-gun back in its holster and took a couple of steps before he drew to a halt, enveloped in a wave of pain which seemed to spread from his thigh to the rest of his body. A mist swam before his eyes and he was barely conscious of Cayuse as the oldster put his arm around his shoulders and helped him limp away.

A day passed, and then another before Marshal Dunbar arrived in Lost Bucket. He had seen enough on his approach to the ghost town to have his worst suspicions confirmed, and he was full of foreboding about what might have happened to Cleadon and Cayuse. He rode his horse through the stream and on down the main street. The silence was oppressive, and his nerves were already jangling when whatever poise he still possessed was shattered by a loud shout:

'Dunbar!'

To hear his name being called was the last thing he had expected, and he was almost too shaken to draw his gun. In another moment he had put it away again as the familiar figure of Cayuse suddenly appeared in front of him.

'Marshal Dunbar!' Cayuse exclaimed. 'Hell's a poppin', what are you doin' here? Never mind. I sure am glad to see you.'

It took the marshal a few moments to gather himself together before he swung down from his horse and tied it to a post.

'Where's Cleadon?' he asked, fearing what the reply might be.

'Right inside. He took a bullet and he can't walk too well, but he's OK.'

The marshal followed Cayuse into the building. Cleadon lay stretched on the floor, his leg swathed in a rough bandage Cayuse had fashioned. He looked up in surprise.

'Marshal Dunbar. I sure didn't expect to see you.'

The marshal stopped in his tracks. As if finding Cleadon and Cayuse was not enough, there was another person present, sitting disconsolately on a broken chair with his arm in a rough sling. It was Cass Ryland. Dunbar turned in bemusement to Cayuse.

'I reckon there's some explainin' to be done,'

the oldster said.

The way Cayuse told it, the story didn't take too long. When he had finished the marshal told his tale and then turned to Ryland.

'You've got a lot to answer for,' he said.

'What they said ain't true,' Ryland replied. 'You'll never be able to prove anythin' against me.'

'That's just where you're wrong. There's enough evidence to put you away for a long time. That is, if you escape the hangman's noose.'

'You figure the case can be proved?' Cleadon asked.

'Sure. Once we get back to Deerwood, there's Crow Jack's evidence plus the evidence of Ryland's man who tried to jump me in Blue Bluff. I'm sure that when we trawl through those newspapers we'll find somethin', not to mention the documents you took from the safe in the bank.'

'I wouldn't look in there if I were you,' Cayuse interposed. The marshal gave him a puzzled glance.

'You'll see soon enough,' Cayuse said.

Dunbar turned to Cleadon.

'Do you think you'll be able to ride any time soon?' he asked.

'Sure. These last couple of days have been enough for me to recover. I don't mind admittin' I was in a pretty bad way, but thanks to Cayuse, I'm OK now. There's one thing that's botherin' me before we think about leavin' though.'

'Yeah. What's that?'